That cut on his f

A deep, jagged slash across his eye outlined the angry skin and still shone red. It wouldn't be long, holed up in his room, and he'd turn into a pale, lifeless hermit, a wasted shell of who he'd been. The other smaller slit that slithered through his upper lip, instead of repulsing her, caused her to dwell on the handsome mouth that had kissed her—that she had kissed back, once so long ago.

He sure had one huge pity party going on. According to Betty, he hadn't even given himself a chance to heal on the inside.

Yet, his eyes had seemed to whisper her name as she moved around the kitchen. Called her so distinctly, she'd whirled around once, expecting to see his lips moving. She saw stone, unyielding and challenging. Barbara longed to catch a glimpse of the same captivating, intense brown eyes that had drawn her in, winked at her, charmed her when she arrived at the Judges' house more than a year ago. They'd danced with mischief, fresh and arrogant, settling in her heart like a wild horse tamed for only a second. Now the gold flecks warned her not to dare come too close.

LINDA S. GLAZ

is a wife, a mother of three and a grandmother of three amazing people. She's been blessed to have a George Bailey life so far. She has been an air force meteorologist. She's taught karate and self-defence for 25+ years. She's directed and sung in church and community theater musicals. When Linda is not writing, she's an agent for Hartline Literary Agency.

LINDA S. GLAZ

With Eyes of Love

HEARTSONG
PRESENTS

 ™ LOVE INSPIRED BOOKS

Recycling programs
for this product may
not exist in your area.

ISBN-13: 978-0-373-48653-3

WITH EYES OF LOVE

www.LoveInspiredBooks.com

Printed in U.S.A.

You are altogether beautiful, my darling;
there is no flaw in you.
—*Song of Solomon* 4:7

The best and most beautiful things in the world
cannot be seen, nor touched…but are felt in the heart.
—Helen Keller

This book is dedicated
to the two most influential women in my life:
Barbara (Bunny) Mapes and Betty (Bets) Henry,
my mother and my aunt, who understood the
true meaning of friendship and unconditional love.

Chapter 1

Elliott flaunted the ring again with diamonds big enough to jam a downspout. He held Barbara at arm's length, surveying her in a way that made her stomach roll. "You want to finish college? Whatever for? You're beautiful, Barbara, and more than smart enough to be *my* wife."

Her eyes snapped open and the vision of Elliott and the vulgar ring disappeared. As she glanced out the car window, Barbara shook her head to clear the memory of their disagreement about her completing her music degree. Oh, well, if he didn't want her to have a career, she could lead a church choir like her mother. After all, marriage was compromise, and it was what she really wanted, right?

A small red and white sign caught against the running board, grazing the side of the family's reliable old Ford. A

Burma-Shave sign—*I proposed*—rode a gust of wind and skipped like a rock across the water. *Water?*

She sat up, a shiver of fear running through her. "Dad, where are we?"

Her father didn't say a word.

Leaning over the front seat, doing her best not to awaken her sisters, Barbara eyed his white knuckles digging into the steering wheel of the family car. Water pushed against the undercarriage, sending them first in one direction and then another. Panic shimmied through Barbara's veins as she stared at the sheets of rain.

Shifting in her seat, she nudged aside her sister, Abby, all the while pressing her nose against the glass like the kids at the toy store window where she worked weekends. Lightning flashed, and before she could blink, thunder shook the sky. It rumbled through the car and through her. Her heart strummed the message in her ears: *This is no toy store.*

"Dad, are we going to be all right? What's happening?"

"Barbara, sit back!" He rarely raised his voice, making her realize how serious the situation was.

Her mother turned in her seat, her mouth tightening into a pencil-thin streak across her face. "Don't disturb your father."

Barbara wriggled back between her two sleeping sisters. Assuming control, she draped an arm around each of her younger siblings and pulled them close. Their steady breathing reminded her to remain calm and not frighten them with her own insecurities. That wasn't easy when fear prickled so expertly along her spine.

Why had they decided to stop for breakfast? Now the buckwheat pancakes rested like thick maple sludge in the pit of her stomach. If only they had stayed on the main road for the last leg of their trip when they had left Georgia and crossed into Tennessee, they would be well ahead of the storm and well on their way back to New Castle, Indiana. Water wouldn't be threatening their lives. Oh, why had Father brought the family on one of his "adventures" at Christmastime of all times? They'd never get back home in time to celebrate with her aunts.

Barbara drew in a deep breath, eased it out. She craned her neck around her sister to look out the window.

After what seemed an interminable spell, a rush of water struck from behind, and the car lurched forward. Her mother screamed. Dot and Abigail jerked awake. Barbara's arms shot out and grasped the front seat, pitching her sisters forward. Pain jolted her shoulders and she longed to be young again, allowed to cry. But she'd be twenty in one month. Her parents expected her to behave like a woman.

Dad sucked in his breath. His hand reached across, restraining her mother as the tires dug into something firm. The front wheels gripped, coming to rest on semisolid ground. Ahead, nothing but water for about a hundred feet. To the sides, nothing but water. Behind them, a veritable lake. Yet beyond the flooded section, the ground rose slightly where a town sat on a shallow plateau like a castle surrounded by an enormous menacing moat.

"What happened?" Abigail cried.

Dot scrambled over Barbara's lap to see, her knees gouging into Barbara's legs. "Are we there yet? Oh, where'd all that water come from?"

The rear of the car swung, unsettling Barbara's stomach. "Dad, what was that?"

He downshifted and inched forward until all the tires caught and the car stopped on a rise. The frightful rocking motion eased. "It's all right. I think we'll be safe now." He let out a breath he must have been holding a long time. "I'm not sure how we got caught in the spillover from that tributary." With a shake of his head, his mustache twitched at the edges. "The storm came up so quickly. But I'm mighty grateful for being here...safe at last."

Barbara trembled. "Where are we?"

"I see a few buildings ahead. New Hope, Tennessee, is on the map—small town just off Lake Nickajack. Storms overflowed her, I guess, or maybe a dam broke and the water pushed us up here. Whatever delivered us to this spot, we'll stay in the car for now and be grateful." And undoubtedly meant only for himself, he mumbled, "Dear Lord, let's hope so. Please keep us safe."

He mopped sweat from his forehead to the back of his neck, smashing his hair against his scalp. When he locked eyes with Barbara in the mirror, he broached a smile. "Sorry to have scared you girls."

Barbara stiffened her spine and hugged Dot closer. "Oh, I wasn't scared." *Much.*

He leaned his arm onto the seat and looked over at their mother. He had to see what Barbara saw—Mama hunched over and frozen in place, clutching the car door. "Listen, here's an idea. If you all stay in the car, I'll try and wade through this, see if there's a dry place to spend the night."

"You...are...not...get...ting out." With her head a flurry of shakes, Mama spoke the same way she addressed the girls when she gave way to anger, which wasn't often.

"You're right, Mary. The water's too high. Best we wait right here for Teddy Roosevelt and his Rough Riders." His lips tipped at the edges, but no one laughed.

Jackson staggered through the water and tapped on the car window.

In the driver's seat sat an older man, disheveled and with panic defining his face, who turned his head at the noise, staring wide-eyed. "What?" Slowly he cranked down the glass.

"Sorry, sir. Didn't mean to alarm you."

"S'all right. Who are you?" His gaze stretched from Jackson to the blanket of water. "How did you get here?"

Jackson nodded up ahead. "If you'll help me pull that rowboat closer, we can get your family into town. It's drier the farther you go." He tugged at the end of a rope and the small craft bobbed. "Good thing you found this rise. I watched a car slide away not ten minutes before I spotted you."

A woman leaned across the seat, resting a shaky hand on the ledge of the door. "Are the people all right?"

Jackson nodded and dipped his head to her level. "Ma'am. Some fellas are working to get those folks out now. South area was hit the hardest. A small dam broke. That's probably what pushed your car here." He pointed ahead of them. "Town sits up away from the flood plain and the water's not so deep. You folks hit the worst of the overflow, but seems like that worked in your favor." He leaned against the car and saw the fearful expressions coming from the faces in the backseat. With a lighthearted glance, he smiled and winked at the three girls through the window.

The biggest one's cheeks flamed red and her back squared like a soldier's. His mom always said a smile could put anxiety to rest.

The girl lifted her nose high.

Or maybe not.

Having twisted her head away from his gaze, she leaned into the front seat where her mother wore a frown. Jackson had no clue how to put this family at ease. He had to get Little-Miss-What's-Her-Name and the rest of the family to safe, dry ground before the water shifted their car again.

* * *

Flirting? Barbara shook her head.

"Girls? Are you all right?" her mother asked.

Reminded to help and not hinder, Barbara's newly found courage told her that she should try and offer comfort, though she could use a dose herself. "We're fine, Mama. Honestly. Aren't we, girls?" Her glance skipped to the reddish-blond curls atop Dot's head and the honey-colored waves of Abigail's, mushed from sleeping so long. Not a word crept through their tight lips.

From the corner of her eye, Barbara stole another peek at the man speaking to her father.

His firm grip on her dad's arm and his reassuring words offered hope. The man's energy and strength were apparent as the thick muscles bulged in his neck when he moved.

Another glance in his direction confirmed what she had observed when he had gaped in the window at her. He had the biggest, brownest eyes she'd ever seen on a man. Solid, that's what her father would say.

She sighed. No, dreamy.

Closing her own eyes for a moment, Elliott's handsome face reappeared, replacing that of the stranger. In her imagination, Elliott's arms surrounded her. Offered her security.

From the time she was a little girl, all she'd wanted out of life was a husband, lots of babies and a chance to sing. She pictured the red and white sign again. *I proposed.* In two more days, she would accept an engagement ring from her handsome beau, Elliott. His parents, the very well-off VanDusens, had planned a huge party for the day after Christmas.

A voice interrupted her. "Miss, I said your father wants you to help him."

Barbara cleared her head. She couldn't think about parties right now. Her lids opened wide, and leaning out the window, she focused on Dad. "Did you call me?"

He turned, inquiring. "What do you think, Barbara? Would you mind?"

The stranger didn't give her the chance to answer. "I'll remain with one of the girls if you want to get your wife into town, or I can get them to town and come back. We can't all go at once."

Mama spoke with her *let's-get-something-straight* voice. "None of the girls will be left behind. Leave me for last."

Dad bent down, patted the hand she'd kept on the window's edge. "Mary, I have to make sure you all are settled. You can't stay because you'll have to take charge of the younger girls in town. Barbara Ruth is hardly a baby. She can be left alone, the girls can't."

"But she—"

"Mary, it's the only way. I'll come right back. Please, don't make this more difficult." He gestured toward the man. "He'll see to Barbara."

The man slipped his wool cap off and rifled fingers through hair plastered to his head with rain. "Ma'am. I'd be happy to—"

"Mama?" Barbara saw growing frustration about to nix any plans of rescue. "I'll be all right. You and Dad get the girls into town." She tried to smile even though she didn't feel all that happy with the decision. "I'll be here. Don't worry." She offered a small chuckle and wave of her arms. "Where else can I go?"

Her father slapped his hands together. "Then let's do this. I'll take the first batch and come back for you two." But worry covered his face.

The stranger turned to him. "Sir?"

"Thomas Richardson's the name."

"I could take them while you waited."

"No. I need to find accommodations. Anyway, allow your arms to rest. Once I have the ladies settled, I'll return."

Abigail, fourteen, sat straighter. "I'm hardly young, Fahther." Her eyes sparkled at the stranger.

"True, but only Barbara will stay."

Abigail huffed in disappointment.

"You'll have to make do with the paddle, Mr. Richardson." The man indicated a sad, worn piece of wood. "That's all I could find. There's a pole in the bottom of the boat if you get stuck."

Barbara cranked the window down the rest of the way. Her father's face tightened. He whispered close to her ear. "You'll be fine, Barbara Ruth. This young man's going to stay by the car."

He *was* upset. The only times he ever called her Barbara Ruth were when he was angry or frightened. His normal nickname for her to this day was Bunny.

"Don't worry about me." She had to work at being convincing.

"All right. Time's awastin'." Her father sounded confident, but his face revealed otherwise. She'd seen that same look when she had overheard him telling her mother how he had to fire one of VanDusen's employees for stealing.

A glance over her shoulder and twinges returned to Barbara's stomach. Left alone with a total stranger and a fresh one at that. Well, she had no interest in his admirable stature, his deep, warm voice, his winks *or* his big brown eyes.

The family gone, Jackson stood guard at the edge of the car to prevent the wheels from sliding. With town just in front of them, they'd arrive in no time, but Mr. Richardson only had one paddle, and then he needed to locate a place for them. And he'd admitted to driving all day. His arms must be plenty sore already.

Four families, so far, had nearly vanished in the swell of water. All afternoon Jackson and two friends had pulled folks out. Now the muscles in his arms cramped against the cold. Grabbing the edge of the window frame, he stretched the kinks from his shoulders and neck. A glance in the window told him the girl was mortified to be left alone with him. And he'd winked at her.

He glanced again through the window as she looked up. Her eyes widened and, once again, she spun away.

Jackson groaned. If he hadn't stopped this last time, he could be home with a cup of strong, hot coffee in his hand while eating biscuits and honey. But then, he wouldn't have been able to live with himself. What man could stand by and watch a car go under? His stomach rumbled and reminded him he hadn't eaten since breakfast. He licked his lips, anxious for the boat's return.

She stirred.

A light tap on the window brought no response. Only her stiff back. Didn't she realize he wanted to help? *Women.*

A slight shift drew his attention to the back fender. The car had slipped ever so slightly to the left. Jackson sprinted to the rear pressing his back into the wheel well. He wouldn't allow her to get hurt. His boots dug in as he pushed with all his might. Sweat coated his underarms despite the cold. He counted to three, stiffening the muscles in his legs, and shoved hard.

He heard the side door crack open and he glanced around. Barbara What's-Her-Name stuck her head out.

"Get inside!"

Her frightened voice sliced through the moist air. "What happened?"

"Not now!" One foot slid into the water, but the other

held. *One...two...three. Give it everything, Jack!* One last
lunge and the car inched forward again. He rose from the
murky ground and made his way around the side.

Before he could pass the back door, it opened wide.
Straight into his gut. He slipped on the slimy ground and
slid into the water. Sludge draped over his legs like heavy
canvas. He struggled to stand, dripping with mud, and
fumed. *Swell!*

Her eyes scoured him. Rivers of mud slopped down
his arms. If anyone had told him this story, he would have
laughed, but not today.

"Can I help?" She offered a hand without leaving the
car.

A frown overtook his face until he feared he must look
like one of the thunderclouds above them. He gritted his
teeth. "I think you have helped quite enough."

Barbara's heart thudded with mortification. "I'm
s-sorry." Her fingers grew clammy as her face heated.

He stared through her. Obviously he didn't have much
of a forgiving spirit.

She heaved a harsh sigh. What a trip this had been.

Barbara ducked back in and slouched against the backseat, fingers to her cheeks. *Count to ten. Mama always
says to count to ten.* Then she recalled Dad's words. "We're
going on a great adventure." Another engineering site
search for the VanDusen company. And Dad always took
his family along. He loved excitement and even a trip to
the store became an adventure to him. Well, this was turning out to be one Cracker Jack of an adventure. Besides,
she was too old for these excursions into the unknown,
and on her Christmas break no less.

As far as she was concerned, life could limp along at
a snail's pace. All she desired at the moment was her ring

from Elliott. Dreamy eyes could go home to whomever cared. She certainly didn't.

A shiver of remorse slithered through her when she remembered she didn't know a thing about this stranger other than that he was saving her family. Only being alone with him next to the swirling water frightened her.

A rap on the roof. She rolled down the window.

"I didn't mean to grouse. You all right in there?"

"Y-yes," Barbara said, chewing the edge of her lip. If truth be known, her heart beat like an African conga; her knees shook so that, if they were maracas, they'd be clacking a tune; and her mind was filled with thoughts of unimaginable horrors that might befall her. Why, this fellow could be a modern-day Jack the Ripper. She rolled the window back up a bit.

Mama was right; she read too many novels. Searching for something to occupy her time, she lifted the suitcases to the seat and stacked them on top of each other. Then she slumped against the seat and tried to twirl a piece of straight brown hair into a fat sausage on her forehead. She'd inherited Mama's straight, dark brown hair—the reason Dad called her his little China doll. Barbara let go of the coil; nothing.

The man's freezing to death for your sake. She rolled the window back down a bit. "Would you like to sit inside?" she asked politely.

He glanced down the front of his clothes. "Probably not a good idea. I should keep an eye out in case…well, we don't want any more surprises, do we?"

Chapter 2

More than an hour passed before Mr. Richardson arrived back at the car with the empty boat. Jackson didn't envy him, limp arms dragging at his sides.

The girl stuck her head out the window, but he noticed she didn't open the door this time. "Dad, is there a place for us in town?"

Mr. Richardson's face smacked of exhaustion as he stretched his neck from side to side, but he didn't show weakness when speaking to his daughter.

"We met up with the mayor, Charles Judge. We're staying with his family."

She stepped from the car and directed her question to Jackson. "Excuse me. Are the Judges nice people? I mean—"

"Salt of the earth." Jackson nodded and smiled. A quick once-over told him she wasn't as young as he'd originally thought.

She placed a hand over her chest. "But nice enough to spend the night with strangers?" Not waiting for an answer, she addressed her father. "Oh, Dad, it's Christmas Eve. Aunt Ina and Auntie Pearl are expecting us. And my party."

Jackson stepped in when he recognized frustration in the man's eyes. "Miss, you won't be going anywhere for a few days. I'm not even sure your car will start again after inhaling all that water. Let's get you out of the wet and cold. You can worry about parties later." Leave it to a female to worry about parties at a time like this.

Her father pulled her close. "We're lucky to be alive, Barbara. And now a family's been kind enough to house us. Let's say no more."

Offering what Jackson hoped to be helpful reassurance, he looked her in the eyes. "They have a daughter about your age. Good people. Won't mind at all that it's Christmas. Just wait and see." He offered his arm.

She brushed it away and sought the headlight for support.

Jackson shrugged his shoulders and addressed her father, "Sir, do you have any suitcases?"

Mr. Richardson indicated the backseat and Jackson opened the door. "Hey, stacked and ready to go. Let's see if we can fit these between us in the boat."

As her father assisted her, it crossed Jackson's mind that a good dunking might do her some good until he recognized that fear had probably birthed her cold behavior.

He settled onto the center seat of the boat and paddled, giving Mr. Richardson's arms a rest. Once the water grew more shallow, the men stepped out and pulled hard to hoist the boat onto firm ground. Miss Uppity looked ahead, staring wide-eyed at the house.

With a groan her father helped her out of the boat. "Here we are. Past the worst of it, sweetie. The town sits high and almost dry."

"I'll get your suitcases, sir." Jackson retraced his steps. He hefted first one and then the other to Mr. Richardson. With only one bag remaining, he stretched and pulled it from the far end of the boat. Turning toward Mr. Richardson, Jackson reached forward, but lost his footing in the mud for the fourth time that day. Arms flailing for balance, the suitcase slipped and soared through the air.

Miss Richardson froze. "No, no, no, no, no!"

Clothes, colorful *and* personal, straddled mounds of muck like flags waving in the wind, announcing her arrival.

Drawing himself off the ground one leg at a time, Jackson's lip quivered, a grin struggling not to cut loose. "Sorry. I sure didn't…"

Every clean and dry thing from her suitcase lay covered in slimy mud. Jaw tight, the girl rushed to gather the personal items he'd exposed to the world. Eyes darting left and right, she scrambled after the garments.

She popped the personal items under her arm with the speed of a lizard snapping a fly.

Once she had managed to snatch the last of her clothes from the ground, she loaded the suitcase and drew herself up. Though her chin tilted high, she listed toward her father. "Shall we go?"

"I can get those cases for you."

Her expression dared him to move before she addressed her father. "Where *are* we going?"

Jackson captured her gaze and nodded ahead. She stared at the house with the winding porch. Her eyes closed, and he sensed with a heaviness in his bones how horrid she felt waiting to face a house full of strangers.

A great deal had occurred since they'd left Georgia that morning: heavy breakfast, horrible storm, flooding, and now, here they were stranded with no other choice than to stay with people they didn't know. *Some adventure.*

Hand grasping the handle tightly, Barbara lifted the suitcase. Water drained from the cracks in pirouetting streams as she narrowed her eyes on the incorrigible man beside her. So much for dreamy eyes.

Drawing herself up, ignoring the brown sludge stuck to her bag, she started the trek toward the house, wet shoes sucking in the smelly mud. If her friends at home could see her, she would never live this down. A trickle on her cheek. She swatted with her free hand and transferred a blob of dirt to her face. Was there no end to the humiliation?

She must look a horror. *Hi, I'm Barbara Richardson. Nice to meet you. No, I don't generally get mud facials in the middle of the day. This is just a special occasion.* The peculiar thought brought an unexpected smile.

Over her shoulder she heard *his* voice. "May I help?"

Smile gone, Barbara gritted her teeth, civility far from her voice. Keeping her gaze straight ahead, a familiar comment came to mind. "I think you have helped quite enough."

"Touché."

A chuckle?

Dad offered his arm and hurried her up the slope. He must have read her thoughts, because one more minute and that man would have some parent's faded memory.

She focused ahead where a chubby teenager lounged on the steps of the large colonial. A green-and-gold striped long-sleeved shirt strained over his frame and his hands continued nonstop plunging from his pockets to his mouth. Fourteen? Fifteen years old? About Abigail's age.

He mucked his way toward them. "Hey there," he shouted. "I'm Willie Judge. C'mon in. My sister'll be out in a minute. She's helping Mother ready things."

Empty peanut shells flickered over his feet like a shower. Of course. Peanut country. Now that she thought of it, the earthy smell of wet dirt and nuts filled the air as if she had a bucketful in her hands. She sniffed; her stomach growled. When she glanced to the left, she spied the end of a long building in the distance, smoke curling from the top. A huge sign on the road read "Judge's Homegrown Goober Peas. Pick a pile and see 'em smile."

Willie smiled all right…and stuffed more in his mouth.

A giggle cracked through her sour mood. Like a chubby panda bear, he ate and ate.

Now that the clothing debacle was over, she needed to make the best of the situation. That meant being grateful—extremely grateful they had a place to stay. She stopped the briefest second and closed her eyes. *Thank You. Forgive me for whining. I know You brought us through what could have been a horrible disaster.*

Soiled clothes could always be washed. Barbara frowned. That foolish man should clean them for her. No, on second thought, having him handle her clothes again wouldn't do at all. Her cheeks warmed anew.

Nearing the house, she spied a young woman. At least he'd been right about that. Barbara guessed her to be eighteen or so. She had come out on the porch, sliding one hand to her brow and waving them in with the other.

As they drew closer, the girl smiled. "I'm Elizabeth Judge."

Dad stepped forward. "Hello, again, young lady. This is my daughter, Bunny."

Barbara intended to offer her hand, and started to, but dirt covered her fingers. She drew back and apologized. "Sorry, nice to meet you." Wiping the mud on her blue gabardine skirt, she breathed out a sigh. "Oh, well, it's already so filthy, one more smudge isn't going to make much difference. I'll have to sponge it."

Elizabeth shook her head. "Don't worry. We're a mess, too. I've been scrubbing floors all morning."

Barbara quaked inside. How ghastly, moving into their home bag, baggage and mud. "And we impose."

Pulling a face, Elizabeth said, "Oh, pfft. We love having company." Her grin told Barbara they'd found a welcome refuge. "Here, let me take that for you." Elizabeth wrinkled her nose as mud slid off the sides of the suitcase. "You'll be needing some soap and water and Mother's clothesline."

More than you realize. "Thank you."

With her free arm looped through Barbara's, Elizabeth pulled her up the steps, avoiding the slippery spots. Willie dashed around them like a bouncing ball.

In no time, Elizabeth leveled a correcting glance in the teen's direction. "William, I'm sure Miss Richardson doesn't need your antics. Go in and tell Mother the rest of our guests are here." She returned her attention to Barbara. "Just call me Betty or Bets, everyone does. We'll get you settled as soon as we can. Mother's in the other room starting a fire to dry your clothes."

Barbara and Elizabeth wiped their feet, though wet feet were the least of the problems. Then they entered a large foyer where wreaths and boughs of greens with bright red bows circled the walls. The smell of pine filled Barbara's nose and elicited pleasant memories, bringing a smile. A long Persian runner, covered with three smaller rugs to catch the mud, ran the length of the hall.

Elizabeth touched her hand. "Bunny?"

"Please. Everyone else calls me Barbara except my dad. Bunny has been his nickname for me since I was little—whether I liked it or not." She glanced over her shoulder to be sure her father had retrieved the last of the luggage. The man with the boat was nowhere to be seen.

Tripping down the hallway toward them, Willie halted.

"Bunny? Did you say Bunny?" And with a startled expression, asked, "Like a rodent?"

"William." An older female voice rose sharply from the other room and he stopped pestering Barbara.

"Now you're going to get it." Betty turned back to Barbara. "Forgive my brother."

He stopped. "Hey!"

Betty looked at Barbara's wet feet. "I'm sorry. I'm chattering away about my foolish brother and you'd no doubt like to change into something dry."

"You're all very kind."

Betty squeezed her arm. "Nonsense. I know this sounds silly—" she glanced at Willie's retreating footsteps "—but I always wanted a sister. I just didn't know I'd be getting one for Christmas."

Barbara liked Betty immediately.

"Don't look so sad. This will be fun." Betty's eyes sparkled. Barbara couldn't help but smile.

Just how pleased would the VanDusens be if uninvited guests showed up on their doorstep as a holiday surprise? Barbara shook her head. That was there and this was here. Two entirely different places, two entirely different circumstances. No fair comparing her future in-laws to anyone else. But still…

Betty giggled and hauled her up the long staircase. "Mother said you'll stay in my room, your parents in the guest room and your sisters can stay in Father's library on the love seats. Grand's in the other guest room, but we have plenty of pillows and quilts. 'Nuff to go 'round."

Now Jackson understood the expression *looked like a drowned kitten*. Because that snooty little thing surely had. He'd bet the bedraggled kitten had claws, too, but he wasn't about to find out firsthand. She'd looked madder than a riled rattler when he had lifted her clothes from the ground. It wasn't like he had tried to fall and drop her suit-case. Just the thought brought his hands to the seat of his pants and he wiped dirt out of the back pockets.

In spite of the long, tedious day, he whistled "We Wish You a Merry Christmas" as he returned to the rowboat. Time to rescue another creature from the swamp. Maybe this one wouldn't be so haughty and unappreciative.

Ignoring the cold fingers of exhaustion gouging his back, he pushed the boat down the slope and into the water. Two fellas waved—the Redfield brothers. Jackson cupped his hands and hollered, "You manage to get those folks out of their car all right?"

John leaned to the edge and shouted back, "We got 'em. They're stayin' with our parents. Mother, father, a baby and an old lady, the mother-in-law, I guess. Ugly enough to be your old hound dog, Simon."

Jackson smiled, remembering that patched-together dog of his youth.

He raised his voice a notch or two. "Well, you treat her like a queen, you hear? Show some charity, boys. It's Christmas."

"Aw, we're always nice, Jack. You're just a Goody Two-shoes. Mama Judge's little boy."

"Yeah, yeah. Merry Christmas. Tell your folks I said hey."

"Will do. By the way, the sheriff says everybody's ac-counted for. We can go home and enjoy some spiked egg-nog."

Not in the Judge house. Mother saw to that.

Jackson sighed with relief. His arms were sore enough for two men. With the last of his strength, he guided the boat along the edge of the water and headed around the west side, where he could tie the boat, climb the hill and check on the factory. As manager, he'd have to keep checking on the building.

Entering by the end door, he spied Ophelia, the barn cat they kept to control the ever-increasing rat and mouse population. She dashed over, purred and rubbed against his leg. "Hey there, girl."

Tall ears, long tail. Good mouser.

Pretty little thing. Bright eyes. Mischievous personality. Whoa. Wait. Barbara Richardson fit that mold. He shouldn't be thinking about *her*.

He straddled a crate, dissecting the last five hours and scratched Ophelia's ears. She flipped on her back and he rubbed her soft, furry belly. That girl might have the slimmest reason to be angry. When he picked her camisole up from the ground, he thought her eyes would bug clean out of her head.

His hands tightened on Ophelia's tummy and she screeched. "Sorry, girl. Didn't mean to be so rough." The petulant princess flipped to her feet like a log in water, lifted her tail and strutted away. He pictured Barbara Richardson: head in the air, suitcase covered in mud, feet slopping up the incline and he laughed—petulant princess is right.

Show some charity. His words to the Redfields rushed back to haunt him. *All right, all right. I'll show some charity. I'm gonna have to, Lord.*

Chapter 3

Barbara breathed in luscious smells. Cinnamon—one of her favorites.

Betty's grandmother brought a tray of tea and cookies from the kitchen and placed them on the side table. Her hands fluttered as she set out plenty of cream and honey for the hot cinnamon tea. "Here we go. Fresh from the oven." Then she disappeared again without saying another word.

"That—" Betty giggled "—was Grand. Grandmother Delaney. She's a wonder. Just taste these warm ginger-snaps."

A loud ruckus rounded the corner in the forms of Willie, Abigail and Dot, who sprinted straight for the treats. Hands grabbing, all three dug in.

"Girls!" Mama and Mrs. Judge entered from the hallway. Mama's hawk eyes honed in on Abigail and Dot and without another word, they replaced the cookies, sat down, crossed their hands in their laps and waited patiently for the refreshments and Mama's chastisement to be served.

Dot's face fell. "We forgot."

Barbara felt for Abby, who knew better at her age. "Sorry, Mama."

What must Mrs. Judge think of them? Willie might have led the charge, but this was his house and her sisters knew better than to behave like hooligans.

A few minutes later when Barbara glanced up from clearing the refreshment tray, Mr. Judge and Dad filled the doorway, their arms loaded with hardwood for the fire. Her father seemed to shrink inside the warm coat Mr. Judge had offered him. At least two sizes too big. Barbara wanted to laugh, but that would be silly, especially since she wore Betty's clean work overalls from the factory. Tall and willowy to Betty's short hourglass figure, Barbara had to make do as the legs rose up her calves, but Betty's dress would have looked even funnier on her.

Her father traipsed to the hearth and stacked his load of wood neatly in the old coal scuttle that served as a wood bin. He brushed the stray pieces of bark onto his hand then into the fire.

Dad turned and stood tall. "Charles, you haven't met this beautiful lady right here. My wife, Mary. We're much obliged to all of you for your kindness. Especially you, Mrs. Judge. I know this means extra work for the mistress of the house."

Mama blushed at Dad's sweet words but Barbara sang inside. How wonderful after all this time to have your husband say you're beautiful. Would Elliott think that of her after more than twenty years?

Mr. Judge rebuttoned his coat and gestured for Willie to follow him. "You get the home fires burning, Thomas, and William and I will go for the tree."

"A tree?" Barbara said.

"We couldn't have you sweet girls missing a visit from Santa, now could we?" Mrs. Judge grinned at Barbara.

Her sisters would be so disappointed to find a tree with no gifts. Even though they didn't believe in Santa Claus, they were especially excited about Christmas.

Barbara's thoughts drifted to the tortoiseshell combs she was certain waited in beautiful wrappings under the tree at home. She remembered staring in the window of Freidmans' Department store in New Castle, begging her mother for them. There would be no presents this year. Not until they got home.

So no one else would notice, she whispered in her father's ear, "Dad. What about…"

He nudged her. "We're warm and safe."

Betty tugged her hand. "Let's take the girls into the parlor. We have red and green construction paper strips and glue all ready to be turned into a garland. That will keep their minds off their adventure for a while."

The girls laughed as the chain stretched longer and longer. Barbara shook her head; the paper chain could circle the town. She stared at the empty space Betty said would house the tree. How beautiful the branches would be with tiny candles and garland covering top to bottom. And a star.

Barbara sat next to her mother and leaned her head against the comforting shoulder. "I hate for Dot to be let down. Abby will understand why there are no presents."

Her mother stroked her head. "They aren't babies anymore, Barbara. None of you are. Why, Dot's almost eleven. We've always taught you girls Christmas is about Jesus."

"I know." Barbara gazed over her shoulder as if she could see her littlest sister in the morning, eyes heavy with disappointment. "We'll have a wonderful Christmas when we get home."

As the door burst open and a blast of chilly air whirled into the house, Barbara drew her sweater around her shoulders. A tall man drenched in rain and dirt trudged backward through the door, supporting the end of an evergreen with Mr. Judge and Willie lugging the top. The smell of pine immediately infused the air.

"You heave and I'll ho," shouted the mayor, laugh lines fanning from his eyes. "We'll get it into the parlor, Jack. Pull. I'm not as young as I used to be, son." His hearty laughter filled the room. "Come on, Willie, help me push this monster in. It must be all of nine feet tall."

Mrs. Judge rushed before them, clearing the way to the parlor. "In here. That's a beauty, isn't it? Oh, Charles, you cut a dandy this year and in such bad weather. Or did you down it, son?"

The men set the tree on the floor. Without a single wobble from the base—perfect.

Barbara glanced over and for the first time realized who "son" was.

Jackson smiled, offered a small salute and another wink. He mouthed a silent *I'm sorry.*

After a long silence, she lifted her head but kept her hands tucked in her coverall pockets. "Nice to meet you, Mr. Judge. Salt of the earth, huh?"

Barbara swallowed hard.

Hair dangling in eyes that danced, Jackson grasped her hand, forcing her to be amiable. "I guess we did meet somewhere. Bunny, huh?" He glanced at Willie. "Like—"

"Don't you dare." She yanked her hand away.

"Jackson!" His mother's voice echoed off the walls. "You should consider helping your father set the tree to rights and not be a tease."

He bowed low. "See you, Miss Richardson. C'mon, sis. Let's decorate this behemoth." He worked his way toward Dot and Abigail, his charisma causing them to shuffle their feet. "Maybe Barbara's sisters would like to join me."

He chucked each of the girls under the chin and smiled that same cocky grin that had the breath trapped like a clogged drain in Barbara's throat.

Abby blushed red as a Christmas bow, but Dot dashed past her, straight to the tree with Willie lollygagging behind. Barbara finally strolled to the love seat and sat on the edge where she watched her sisters help arrange the glass balls for the tree.

Abigail cried, "Whoever saw a glass peanut before?"

Willie's ears turned red.

Giving in to the festivities, Barbara began looping strips of red and green ribbon through the ornaments' clasps. As she handed them over, she couldn't miss Jackson's stare.

His eyes followed her every step. If this kept up, she'd need to have a word with him and make him stop the nonsense. She was practically a married woman.

Jackson couldn't help but notice Barbara's hearty appetite. Ham, sweet potatoes, creamed peas, biscuits with honey butter, apple pie and icy eggnog. Had she saved room for dessert?

She avoided eye contact, avoided him in general. So that was how she planned to play the game? Pretend he didn't even exist? Well, he'd see about that.

After supper, they all struggled through the mud to attend Christmas Eve service. More than enjoyable, Barbara even found enough charity to smile at Jackson in a moment of weakness when the Baby Jesus jumped out of the manger and cried for his mama. Mary and Joseph chased the toddler the entire length of the aisle while the whole church rocked with laughter. But it was his "Mama, I wet!" that sent the parishioners over the top.

Jackson jumped from the pew and belly-laughed as he scooped the boy into his arms and returned him to Mary.

Barbara's eyes took in the scene for so long that Jackson grew a bit uncomfortable with her scrutiny. Was the icy beauty thawing a little?

His heart hammered when her voice rose above everyone else's during "Angels We Have Heard on High." She *sang* like an angel.

Back at the house again, she crossed through the entrance ahead of her parents to cheers from Betty. What now? Betty never missed a chance to play a prank, usually on Jackson or Willie. Maybe he'd be lucky and she'd aim her antics at their visitor for a change.

Betty pointed up. "Look. You're under the mistletoe, Barbara." Then, she shoved Jackson from behind and her eyes lit up like Fourth of July sparklers. "Go on, Jack. *Kiss* her."

His face warmed, but the idea didn't exactly repulse him.

Barbara shrank inside her coat and stepped back, nearly toppling her mother. *Oh, Betty, stop.* Why, he barely knew her. She licked lips that had grown dry and looked around for an escape. To pass through to the other room, she had no choice but to cross under the mistletoe. Maybe if she sprinted for the stairs.

With the lightest touch above her elbows, his hands circled her arms. "Barbara, it looks like we're trapped." He chomped a piece of licorice-smelling gum.

Oh, no.

The scent of pine stuck to his clothes; flutters filled her stomach. A protest wouldn't come to her lips once she looked into those coffee-brown eyes. What was happening to her? She actually wanted him to kiss her, and she closed her eyes anticipating warm lips.

Softer than silk, he pecked her on the forehead.

On the forehead?

Barbara's eyes flew open.

Of course, she had no right to kiss anyone other than Elliott and even then…

Barbara kept her gaze leveled at Jackson. No more funny business.

She marched to the piano and launched into a rousing "Jingle Bells," showing off her voice a bit more. Well, maybe a lot more.

After the singing, while everyone else finished the walnut cake Betty's grandmother had baked, Barbara tugged a light sweater around her shoulders and strolled onto the porch. The cool air engulfed her. Stars, unbelievably bright, twinkled overhead and Barbara wondered. Could Elliott be enjoying the same starry night? Did he search for the Christmas star on Christmas Eve like she and her sisters did? Funny how many details she didn't know about Elliott's faith.

Friends from childhood, she and Elliott had fished together and climbed trees until he had discovered she was a girl. From young friends to an engaged couple.

But was that enough to base a relationship on? She sighed. There wasn't a Mr. Rochester for every young Jane aspiring to theatrical romance. Few people she knew had a marriage like her parents. And if she didn't love Elliott deeply at the moment, she would in time. He was the most eligible bachelor in town—a sensible match. When it came to marriage, it was good to be sensible, wasn't it?

A balmy breath streamed past her ear. Without thinking she whispered, "El? Is that you?" Pirouetting on her heel, she half expected him to be there. The voice was different. Deeper. Warmer than Elliott's. And the face more rugged than Elliott's.

Jackson's searching eyes reflected the sparkling stars. He fingered a stray lock on her forehead. "Your hair is lovely."

"It is?" Her heart thumped against her ribs like a metronome set on *presto*. Her body fought every ounce of her good sense. Why did he affect her like this?

He leaned toward her, brushed his lips over her mouth and she found her own lips responding. They pulled away from each other.

He still fingered a strand of her hair, then said, "It would look lovely in combs like Grand's."

"What?"

"I mean." Open mouth, insert a big boot.

Jackson's hands circled her shoulders, steered her to look at him again. "Not that you look like Grand."

She pulled back and stared. "Well I should hope not. She's a lovely lady but—"

"But she's older than Adam and Eve?" He grinned. "I meant you'd look lovely with combs in your hair. I'm… trying to pay you a compliment."

His face grew hot, no doubt red as a Christmas apple. Pointing to the porch swing, he said, "Please sit down. I owe you more than one apology."

She settled onto the cushion.

"I've started out on the wrong foot if truth be told."

"Wrong foot?"

Holding up his hand, he shook his head and scrambled for the right words. "There's little more I can say other than I'm truly sorry for everything today."

"I could say the same. After seeing my clothes on the

ground, I'm afraid I put you at the top of my *list,* as Mother calls it. And not a list you want to be on."

"Heaven help me." She softened ever so slightly and he pushed on. "You have a lovely voice, by the way. A distinctly trained sound."

"That's what I've been attending school for. Voice. Until recently I thought I might try opera."

"Lofty ideals."

"Indeed. But last semester ended all that silliness." Her face fell and he couldn't imagine what would stand between this woman and her dreams.

"How so?"

"Oh, you don't want to hear about me."

He leaned toward her, rubbed his hand along her arm and she didn't pull away. "I'd like to hear all about you."

She chewed the edge of her lip, offered him a *please lean forward and kiss me again* look, but immediately pulled back.

What was going on in that beautiful head of hers? "Listen, I didn't mean to overstep my bounds."

Her face shot doubts in his direction.

She lived far away and if he didn't try, he'd lose this beautiful woman he'd come to respect and care about in just a short time. How that had happened, he didn't know, but it had.

"Barbara, I need to tell you how I feel."

Face forlorn, she pushed against him and rose from the swing.

He stood next to her. "What's wrong?"

"Jackson. Since it's unlikely we will ever see each other again, let me apprise you of my situation."

Back to the games? He leaned against the porch rail and sucked air through his teeth. "Apprise me? You're going

to *apprise* me of your situation? What does that mean?"
He chuckled.

She planted her feet as if her knees might give out. "It
means you can stop flirting. I am engaged to be married
to Elliott Grayville VanDusen, son of the New Castle Van-
Dusens." With a huff, she blew the bangs out of her eyes.

Laughter bubbled in his belly. "VanDusen? Is that a
real name or one you made up?" His brow furrowed as
his eyes slid to her finger. "So where's your ring, future
Mrs. VanDusen?"

Her lips pursed. "I'll have you know, I'm getting the
ring for Christmas. And yes, it most certainly is a real
name. If you'll excuse me." She gritted her teeth and
pushed past him toward the house.

He grabbed her arm. "Is that why you've given up your
own dreams?"

She cleared her throat. "It's none of your business. I
want to be married. I can't wait to be married. In a year
and a half, I will be married to Elliott Grayville—"

"VanDusen." A low whistle escaped his lips. "Oh," he
called out. "The *New Castle* VanDusens. My mistake."
Jackson curbed the rest of what he longed to say.

She hurried to the front door without looking back, but
she did offer the last word. "Disdain, like my dreams, I
can live without."

She stomped through the door. He rifled fingers through
his hair. But why should she have to give up her dreams?
Just to marry a VanDusen?

In the morning, the adults stumbled to the parlor with
sleep-filled eyes, and Barbara couldn't help but notice how
exhausted Mr. and Mrs. Judge appeared. Stockings hung
by the fireplace for everyone, Barbara included, and she
was encouraged by Betty's incessant clapping to plunge

her hand inside hers. Peanuts and oranges greeted her fingers and something small lay at the bottom in a piece of tissue paper. She drew her hand out. A beautiful silver pin, etched on one side with the tiniest stone in the middle. She was sure she had seen one just like it on top of Betty's jewelry box when they had folded her clothes earlier, but she'd never be rude enough to ask.

Jackson sat unusually quiet. She'd hurt him. What did he expect? Declaring his love for her after one day? She was marrying Elliott. And that was that.

She glanced up as the Judges presented her parents with a twenty-five-pound bag of roasted peanuts to take home for their gift. Her father slapped his knee and said, "Say, but won't our neighbors be jealous. Thank you so much."

When most of the younger folks' gifts had been opened—and there had been an excess—a small box found its way into Barbara's hands.

"For you," Betty whispered.

For Barbara from The Elves.

"What? Oh no. Christmas is for children."

"Look around, we're all children for the day."

After some coaxing, Barbara pulled the bow off, slid the paper aside and opened the gold box. Inside lay two silver and pearl combs. When she looked up, she thought she caught the slightest glint from Jackson's eyes. She was convinced he knew who they were from. Probably Betty. Maybe they'd been intended for their grandmother making them all the more dear to her.

"I don't know what to say."

Jackson, long legs stretching, leaned back, his hands tucked behind his head. "I'll bet that's a first."

"Jackson!" After his mother leveled the stern reproach,

startling him, his chair slipped out from under him and he fell over backward.

Merry Christmas, Barbara.

Chapter 4

April 1942

Sound carried up the stairs. The radio. More bad news for the home front.

Barbara tilted her head to one side. Had she heard right? Another local boy dead? Chester Someone-or-other. The name sounded familiar. A boy she'd probably gone to school with.

The announcer repeated the name and realization dawned: Kathy Pennington's younger brother. Why, he was just a kid. Freckle-faced Chester, the boy who had played the violin for the Ladies' Sunday Tea.

She collapsed on her bed in tears. Poor Kathy. Barbara had to do something to help the war effort. The Women's Auxiliary ran the USO. Said they didn't think it appropriate for the young women being around strange men. And rolling bandages every other Saturday wasn't enough.

She sucked in a life-renewing breath. Closing her door against the news, she escaped reality for a few minutes more while she glanced at the suitcases on her bed. For a month there would be nothing but Betty's wedding. Happy times. Pleasant things to think about.

Folding the last sweater and plopping it into her bag led her one step nearer New Hope, Tennessee. Her case, almost full to the top, had just enough room for the wedding gift before latching the lid. She couldn't wait to see Betty's face when she opened the small box and found the matched Breitling watches her uncle had sent from Switzerland. She'd wanted a very special gift, since she and Betty had become best friends over the last year and a half through letters. Lots and lots of letters.

Lifting the top note from her drawer, she read, again, the opening line. *Barbara, I have the best news.* With a smile, she pictured Betty, hands clapping, dancing around, showing off her engagement ring. Just after Christmas, the letter had come inviting her to stand up as maid of honor. Once upon a time, she might have been asked as matron of honor. But Elliott Grayville VanDusen hadn't been a firecracker like she had thought, but a dud, squelching her dreams one by one until the engagement was over.

She plunked down on her bed, moved the suitcase to the side. The catch gave with a thunk. She'd need to tie it closed with a length of rope.

Barbara drew a photo from her nightstand. She and Elliott, last New Year's Eve. The photographer at the restaurant had snapped their picture. She could still feel the coolness when Elliott slipped the ring on her finger. A diamond big enough for three settings. Ostentatious or not, she'd been very happy. Then, when he had demanded she give up singing with the Cincinnati Opera Hall to which she'd been invited for a season, she realized her needs would never be part of their married life. And even though she chose at last to teach rather than perform, she did it because she wanted to, not because it was demanded of her.

She heaved a sigh. But that was then.

Why all the sad recollections? She would soon be in the home of the Judges, a welcome guest, helping with plans for Betty's wedding. She chewed her lip. A bit of envy overwhelmed her as she thought of her own wedding that didn't happen. But it had been her decision. And she knew the honest reason why Elliott hadn't lived up to her expectations. Jackson Judge. She hadn't dared to ask Betty about him in her letters. Now she wished she had.

"Hey, Bun," her father shouted from downstairs loud enough to be heard through the closed door. "Let's get a move on. We'll be late for your train."

Once they arrived at the station, she received another round of last-minute instructions.

Dot ran up and kicked a pebble, acting shy all of a sudden. "Will you bring—"

"A gift for each of you? You know I will. Be good, sweetie."

Abby, pushing sixteen and quite the lady, cleared her throat. "Don't forget. Be sure and punch my pen pal in the arm for me."

"Willie Judge?" She clipped the end of Abby's nose. "You sure you want me to punch him?"

Abby's face glowed red as she turned away.

The train whistled the final *All aboard* and Barbara blew her last kisses. She boarded the train and located her sleeping compartment with no difficulty, and after putting her bags aside, her mind drifted to food. Too excited to rest, she ruffled her new salon-bought curls with her fingers in front of the small utilitarian mirror and changed into a light sweater. *Better.* She padded to the club car and stepped in.

Full.

A matronly woman with salt-and-pepper waves glanced up from a cup of coffee and gestured to the spot next to her. "Over here."

Barbara hustled to the narrow table before someone else had the same idea.

"Have a seat." The woman offered a gloved hand. "I'm Agatha McHale. My husband's gone to lie down and I'm alone, taking up too many seats, I'm afraid. But I need my evening coffee. Puts me in the right frame of mind."

Barbara settled in and raised her hand to get the waiter's attention.

Without waiting for an introduction, the woman said, "We're returning home from visiting our son."

Barbara removed her jacket and placed it on the seat. "He lives out of state?"

"Wounded at Pearl Harbor." She stopped talking and her hand shook when she picked up the cup. Barbara didn't say a word while Mrs. McHale composed herself.

The woman set the cup down and wiped her lips. "We're fortunate he's even alive. We've been traveling for days, but it was worth the time just to see his precious face." She paled, a hand covering her heart. "If only he could see ours."

Barbara wasn't sure what words would comfort more than, "I'm sorry."

"But the doctor has hope. Our son will have to stay in the military hospital until they determine whether or not he'll see again." Tears dotted her plump cheeks.

Barbara patted her hand and offered a hankie she drew from her pocket. "We can't ask for more than that. If it's all right, I'll pray for him." Her mind wandered to Chester.

The woman nodded her head and shook her finger at Barbara. "Now dry that tear."

Barbara reached up and found her cheek damp.

The woman forced a smile. "Life must go on, as my mother used to say. Listen to me. Where are my manners? What's your name, dear?"

"Barbara Richardson." When Barbara looked up, a gentleman had appeared and waited patiently for her order. "Roast beef sandwich and a glass of milk, thank you." She eased back toward the woman. "You said there's hope, though, right? I'm sorry for your sadness."

The woman sat straighter. "If sad things didn't happen, how would we know when times are good? All things happen for a reason, and all things work together for the good for those who love the Lord. Don't you believe that? Why, there's a reason we're sitting right here at this moment. Because you came to sit with me, my boy, a total stranger to you, will be prayed for."

"I never thought of it that way." She glanced up to see her sandwich and milk arriving. Pulling fifty-five cents from her wallet, she smiled her appreciation to the waiter. "Thank you so much."

After a lengthy explanation to Barbara with too many details about her son and how he had been injured, the woman sighed and leaned against the seat. Barbara took a sip of milk as Mrs. McHale's swollen eyes closed and lashes fluttered. "Thank you. I'll sit here a few more minutes. Can't let Mr. McHale see tears. You won't forget to pray?"

"By name every day. You're going to hear good news. I just know it."

Neck muscles taut, the food felt like thick balls of paste stuck in Barbara's throat. She washed down two bites with milk but couldn't finish, so she excused herself.

Reading a few pages of her new book back in her berth, her lids grew heavy. The hero's eyes turned into the wide laughing brown eyes of Jackson Judge. Betty's letters hadn't mentioned Jackson. Maybe he'd moved on and the family wasn't happy with his choices. Maybe he'd married some poor girl—a total stranger he had snatched a kiss from under the mistletoe when her mama wasn't there to protect her. *Oh. Forget about him.*

Her eyes flew open. His being unavailable *was* possible. He might be married with a litter of kids. One in the mother's arms, two hanging on his leg, and another expected any second. Well, not in a year and half, but still, he could be married.

Wouldn't Betty have said something, though?

There was a soft knock on the door.

"Go away, sis. I said I wasn't hungry."

Jackson flopped onto his pillow. Just a bit of peace and quiet, that's all he asked for anymore. All he wanted.

Well, not all.

He tugged the worn photo from his pocket. Dad had used his Brownie camera to take the picture of Barbara and Betty playing in the snow on Christmas day a year and a half ago. He licked dry lips, staring at the two loves of his life. One, a short nuisance, the other, tall and svelte…and beautiful. Out of reach. After all, wasn't this the summer she was supposed to be getting married to Elliott VanDusen of the New Castle VanDusens?

He closed his eyes, hoping to dream.

But it was silly to dream. Dreams were for children, not grown men who had to face facts.

As the train pulled into New Hope, Barbara wiped moisture from the window and stared out, longing for a glimpse of the Judge family. Would Betty remember what she looked like? After all, she wore her hair a lot shorter and curlier than before. And she'd matured. At least she liked to think so.

She reread the copy of the letter from the Cincinnati Opera Hall. They had received her information and would let her know if they were interested in her auditioning. The Opera Hall!

A sigh tore through her. *La Traviata*.

She was careful to wipe her fingers so she wouldn't get carbon copy on the beautiful white skirt and blouse her mother had bought for the trip. The sailor look was all the rage now.

Eyes squinted, she searched the waiting crowd on the platform. Flags waved from eager hands as a horde of families watched, no doubt for their military sons and fathers.

Barbara craned her neck first in one direction and then the other. But no Judges. Wait. There they were, hidden behind a stout lady with a huge hat. Betty, her father and her mother peeked around gaudy blue feathers. Barbara grabbed her handbag and hurried from the train.

"Over here, Betty." She waved until they saw her.

Darling Betty with her dancing blond curls and lovely, almond-shaped blue eyes rushed to Barbara's side. "We didn't think you'd ever get here. Twenty minutes late." She leaned in close and whispered, "I chewed a nail."

"Betty. If that's the worst you—"

"We're glad you're here, dear." Mrs. Judge stepped from behind the feathers and hugged Barbara. "Let's get you home and you can rest up from your trip."

A young man accompanied them, not Jackson. Willie? So tall now, like his brother, and he'd lost the baby fat. He must be seventeen now. "Look at you, Willie."

He cleared his throat. "Will."

"Okay, Will. You're almost as tall as Jackson."

Everyone grew quiet until Betty said, "Will, do you think you could help Dad with Barbara's luggage? Which are yours, Barbara?"

So, Willie now went by Will. It suited him, looking every bit like his brother. If Abigail could see her pen pal now…

In no time at all Mr. Judge located Barbara's luggage and she encamped in the mayor's car. Betty on one side, Mrs. Judge on the other, and Will in the front with Mr. Judge. They all commenced talking at once. An almost nervous jabbering.

Barbara was sorry to be reminded Mrs. Delaney had passed away a year ago.

"We all have a time to be here and Grand lived a wonderful life, full of family and joy." Betty smoothed her skirt.

Barbara squeezed her arm, realizing the truth in those words.

"Barbara, wait 'til you see my gown. It's so beautiful plus Mother's flowers from her greenhouse. Oh, I'm so glad you're here."

Mrs. Judge patted her leg and smiled. "Betty has talked of nothing else. We're so happy you could come, aren't we now?"

"And Jackson?" Barbara forced the smile. "Has he married and moved away like all good sons do?"

Betty's forehead creased. Her lids fluttered, hands trembled, and Barbara wondered what she'd said. Mrs. Judge drew in a shaky breath and stared out the window.

When they arrived at the house, Mrs. Judge instructed her husband in the placement of the luggage.

"Would you like something to eat first, or a rest?" She smiled as if she already knew the answer.

Barbara felt her cheeks warm. "Well, I don't suppose you've forgotten my appetite. I'm hungry."

Mrs. Judge grinned. "We'll get you fed in a jiffy."

There still seemed to be something in the air. While everyone smiled, the undercurrent said all was not right. Following a delicious light lunch where artificial happiness accompanied dessert, she trounced into Betty's room, ready to unpack.

"Bets, is Jackson all right?" Barbara sat on the edge of the bed.

Perched on the ruffled bench in front of her vanity, Betty toyed with a broken bracelet.

"What's going on here? Everyone's acting funny."

Barely looking her way, Betty's eyes strayed to another place altogether. "He joined the service."

"But that's wonderful. So many—"

"No, you don't understand." She held fingers to her lips with one hand and waved Barbara closer with the other. "Could you close the door?"

Barbara rose, gently pulled the door to the bedroom shut and crossed to where Betty sat. She rested a hand against the quivering shoulder. "What happened?" Instantly, the thought of some other girl under the mistletoe seemed irrelevant. Had he been killed? Her hand flew from Betty's shoulder to her own chest. No.

"He was in one of the many explosions in Pearl Harbor."

Barbara gasped. Pearl Harbor? "Is he…did he…oh, Betty, is he all right?" She grabbed Betty and shook her shoulders. "What happened to your brother?"

"Barbara. He's not well."

"I—I didn't know." Her heart flooded with her friend's tears and drummed an increased rhythm in her temple. "Is he in the hospital? Still in Hawaii?"

"He's here. In his room." She drew back, wiping her

eyes with the backs of her hands. "He won't come out until we all go to bed at night. Said he doesn't want our pity. He thinks he's a freak. Some come back...not themselves."

"But your wedding?"

Betty reached for a hankie on her nightstand. "Has no intention of attending. Teddy asked him to stand up with him before Jack left for Hawaii and he agreed he would, but not now. He told Father he won't come down at all." She hiccuped another sob. "I've seen him once since he came home. The day he arrived on the train."

"Well, we'll see about that." Barbara rose, but Betty jumped up and blocked her way.

"No. You can't. Father says he needs time. Please, Barbara. Don't try and force him. Come on. Let's spend the afternoon in the greenhouse picking out flowers for the wedding."

Chapter 5

Tossing in her bed, Barbara experienced one nightmare after another. She pictured Jackson. Burn scars covered a body deformed by injuries. He slumped in his bed, oblivious to the world about him. Then suddenly the dream changed and he was in a small boat calling to her from a large body of water. The ocean. Or the overflow he'd saved them from. One quick wink from his eye and under the water he went again.

She awoke with a start.

Perspiration covering the neck and back of her flannel nightgown, she sat up. Slipping quietly into her robe and fuzzy mules, she padded across the floor. Perhaps warm milk would bring on sleep. Barbara slid the bedroom door open slowly so she wouldn't disturb Betty. She listened for noises downstairs. Not even a mouse squeaked.

Her footsteps slid lightly along the treds, the wood rail smooth under her fingers. She loved the memories of this house, of the time the Judge family had rescued them. She looked up when she stepped off the landing. The doorway at the end of the hall where mistletoe had hung. Jackson's lips, briefly soft and warm on her forehead. A shiver propelled her forward.

Light escaped the bottom edge of the door to the kitchen. She pushed it open, expecting to discover Mrs. Judge hard at work.

"Jackson?"

Must be Betty's friend, What's-her-name.

Who was Jackson kidding? He knew her name. Had tripped it off his lips dozens of times in his mind and around his heart.

Too late to run; instead, he pictured himself a ticket taker selling one admission to the circus sideshow. Well, she could have a good look. One glimpse of his scars and she'd be horrified. She'd run back to New Castle as fast and far as her legs would take her.

For over a year he'd remembered with unusual clarity the dark-haired, blue-eyed beauty who God had delivered to their door on Christmas Eve. Saying, *Here you go, Jackson. Just for you.* He looked the direction of the hallway, remembering when she had stood under the mistletoe. He licked his lips and leaned his arms on the kitchen table.

Now, after one glance at him, she would run, repulsed, and he could go to his room, content there would never be a Barbara Richardson in his life. His hand balled at his side. There was no God caring about his needs. She was someone else's prized possession. Elliott-Rich-Somebody.

He heard a gasp, or was it a sigh? Easing out of his chair, he twisted around, holding out his arms in a gesture that asked, *What are you staring at?*

Her eyes raked him from head to toe. "Hey."

He dug a knuckle into his thigh as his lip curled. "Hey, yourself. Wondered how long before curiosity would get the best of you." She didn't have to say a word. He'd seen that expression before on too many sympathetic faces. "Well? What do you think? You can go back to New Castle now and report you've seen the latest addition to the New Hope Circus. Step right up, two looks for a dime."

"My, but you're taken with yourself, Mr. Judge." Barbara pulled her robe closer, offered him her back and strolled to the refrigerator. Pulling out the pitcher of milk from supper, she closed the door and swirled on her heel. "I came down for a glass of warm milk so I could sleep."

She crossed the floor and withdrew a small saucepan from the cupboard. After pouring in the milk, she lit a match for the burner. She returned to the refrigerator, pitcher in hand—a hand, he noticed, that shook. Repulsed, no doubt, by his looks.

He took a step forward and said, "Just remember, curiosity killed the cat."

Barbara turned, hair flipping into her eyes so he couldn't see them very well. "Then, I guess I'm safe. I'm a rodent after all." With a grin she reached her hand up and pushed the pesky curls aside.

There they were. The prettiest blue eyes he'd ever seen. And she exhibited a more mature charm than the last time she'd graced their home. She'd been sort of a skinny teenager, albeit a pretty one, on her last visit. And now she possessed the poise of a beautiful woman. He wished their situation could be different. Well, that was a dream that could never come true.

As she passed by a second time, he reached for her arm and spun her around to face him. "Say something. Anything."

Her weight eased to one side and she stared from his

face to his hands and back again with a taut expression, one he convinced himself meant outright rejection. Silence stretched, echoing off the walls of the kitchen until she finally said, "Look at you. You never were as handsome as you thought you were. Conceited and fresh, that's all. And why should I care whether you're a clod or the Prince of Wales?" She twirled away and tripped to the stove. He looked at her left hand. No ring.

But his blood boiled before the milk could. Then he sat down in one of the kitchen chairs with his arms crossed, unsure what to make of this girl—this woman. "You haven't changed."

A hiss spat from the stove. Apropos.

"Nor you." She lobbed a glance his direction, staring him in the face with more than sympathy.

That was good; he didn't need sympathy. He scrutinized her finger again. Nothing. "Is that so?"

She swept to the cupboard again, took a cup down and transferred milk from the pan. "Would you like some?" she asked without turning around.

He leaned his back against the chair rail that ran the length of the kitchen until the legs of the chair teetered. His mother's reproach resonated, but he continued to rock. "You are as irritating as ever. Are you Barbara VanSomething yet?"

Her palm slapped the edge of the ceramic sink and she flexed her fingers. "No. You can gloat now. I'm not a VanDusen. And I'm not going to be." She glanced over her shoulder, her brows knitted together. "Do you want milk or not?"

"Not hungry."

She spun around so fast, cup in hand, she almost spilled the contents. "And you'd never think to be sociable."

No longer amused, he tensed and the muscle along his

jaw twitched as he ground his teeth. He realized his eyes showed anything but hospitality, yet, at that particular moment, who cared? "I didn't invite you. I'm not sure why Betty did."

"Because Bets and I are friends. We both appreciate what friendship means. You might take a lesson from her as if you'd been taught manners at some point in your life. In fact—"

He jumped from his seat and grabbed her wrist. "Not another word." Inhaling sharply, he thought better of what he'd planned to say, and let go of her hand. She would not be allowed to burrow under his skin. Because if he allowed even a bit of her to get to him, he would want her in his life forever.

He straightened his shoulders, glared into her eyes and whispered, "I was just on my way to bed, Barbara. Don't s'pose I'll see you before you leave, so have a safe trip home." He stopped in the doorway. "And find another Elliott. Be happy."

Jackson closed the door softly as he probably did every night not to draw attention to himself. Barbara sat down hard, the delicate rose-covered cup shaking as she moved her hand to the table. Her heart hammered, breath hitching in her chest until it escaped at last in one long groan. What a shame he had chosen this path for his life.

That cut on his face and those burns! A deep, jagged slash across his eye outlined the angry skin and still shone red. It wouldn't be long, holed up in his room, and he'd turn into a pale, lifeless hermit, a wasted shell of who he'd been. The other smaller slit that slithered through his upper lip, instead of repulsing her, caused her to dwell on the handsome mouth that had kissed her once so long ago.

He sure had one huge pity party going on. According

to Betty, he hadn't even given himself a chance to heal on the inside.

Yet, his eyes had seemed to whisper her name as she had moved around the kitchen. Called her so distinctly, she'd whirled around once, expecting to see his lips moving. She saw stone, unyielding and challenging. Barbara longed to catch a glimpse of the same captivating, intense brown eyes that had drawn her in, winked at her, charmed her when she had arrived at the Judges' house more than a year ago. They'd danced with mischief, fresh and arrogant, settling in her heart like a wild horse tamed for only a second. Now the gold flecks warned her not to dare come too close.

He *had* changed—by choice.

Heart rate returning to normal, she sipped more of the soothing warm milk. Tasteless. He wasn't approachable, not like this.

His burns and cuts didn't matter. The outside of a man didn't make him attractive. Not really. The brown, expressive eyes pulled her into his sphere where handsome existed from the inside out.

Did he have any hope left at all? The Judge family practiced a deep faith, she knew that of them, but Jackson seemed to have lost his. The newsreels, so far removed from her life, made her realize he had not only endured the realities, but had carried them in his heart where faith once lived.

The last drops of milk swirled in the bottom of the cup. She rose to the sink, poured the rest of the milk out, washed her cup and placed it upside down in the drainer. Then she turned and leaned against the counter, arms crossed. There must be something she could do.

Early Monday morning, the sound of a hammer ringing in the air pulled Jackson from sleep. He stole to the back window and spied his father building the gazebo he was supposed to have built. Not now. No, sir. Not on your life. He would never again go out in the daytime for everyone to gawk and laugh at. *Come on over, folks. Scare the little children for the better part of a nickel.*

His room, a few good books and memories. That was all he had left now. All he needed. He dropped his hand and the curtain flapped against his cheek.

Just leave me alone and lemme sleep. When he was asleep—sometimes—his mind didn't rewind the newsreel called Pearl Harbor. He blasted his fist against the wall.

Seated on the edge of the bed, Jackson stretched and ran calloused fingers through his hair. He was useless. Couldn't even pop a hole in the wall. And at the factory, Father had hired a man, Fred Brady, to replace him. What had he expected? He didn't want the job anymore. Father needed someone to supervise the employees, and Fred was the only available man under seventy-five and over fifteen with no plans for joining the army.

What kind of life was Jackson living? Reaching into his nightstand drawer, he pulled out a pack of gum. Mint. Not his favorite. But you had to actually *go* to the store if you wanted to buy something.

Fred Brady. The guy didn't know the factory. Only how to yell at people and expect more than they could give. Fred didn't manage, he bossed. There was a huge difference.

The only other choice, and the one his father wanted, was Jackson himself. No way would he go back to work in public. And now, he was nothing more than a mooch, a drain on the family's finances. Not for long. Once Betty left on her honeymoon, he'd set things right.

Barbara glanced around to be sure no one saw her lingering outside Jackson's door. She heard him stirring inside. A loud thump shook the wall, then nothing. There was plenty she wanted to say. *Plenty.* But Betty had warned her to leave Jackson alone. While leaning her head to the door, she rapped lightly. Maybe he'd invite her in.

And maybe not.

She tapped again and whispered through the crack, "I know you're in there. I can hear you. Come out and help your father. You might have your family hoodwinked, but you can't fool me."

"Go away."

"Oh, that's original. I'll bet they've heard you say those words at least a dozen times. Well I'm not your family. How about if you pitch in, pull your share of the load? Betty's wedding is in three weeks and your father could use your help."

"No one needs me. Especially my family. Now, leave me be."

She stood quietly for a few seconds before her face warmed and the blood made a rushing sound in her ears. She dug fists into her pockets to keep from battering the door down. The longer she stood there, the more his words registered. *No one needs me. Leave me be.*

"Jackson Judge, stop feeling sorry for yourself and get out here." She whipped her hand out of her pocket and sent a woodpecker's tap against the door.

No noise inside the room.

"Fine, stay there and have your pity party. See if I care. What's horrid is that you don't give a hoot about Betty's feelings. I'm ashamed to know you." She turned her back.

Leaning over the banister, she calmed down before joining the others. Then questioned her next move. She could do more coercing, but she obviously wasn't as good as her mother in the guilt department.

The door behind her creaked. She held her breath, afraid

if she turned and saw him, he'd retreat into the bedroom. A hand gripped her upper arm. She jumped and squealed.

He held her so she couldn't face him. "What are you doing in Will's clothes?" The words hissed in her ear.

Barbara stiffened, her cheeks hot now, her eyes narrowed. "I beg your pardon. They aren't Will's clothes. I like pants, so I wear them." She struggled against his grip and finally pivoted to face him. "I think they're quite..." she looked into his eyes "...handsome." Her heart fluttered. *Say something. He'll notice you staring.* "I can move comfortably in them and do hard work. Stuff I couldn't do in a skirt."

His hand tightened until it pinched her arm like a vise. He scowled. "You look ridiculous. What next? Gonna go to Detroit and work in a defense factory?"

She looked down her nose at his grip and he loosened up. "I might have expected you to be narrow-minded. You can't hurt my feelings, Jackson. I'm secure with who I am and I like wearing slacks when I work." She had her head raised so high, her neck smarted. "Sometimes even when I'm not working. And let's face it, right now women keep the war machines moving along. Don't impugn their efforts."

His brows lowered and his eyes stared with an eerie darkness she hadn't noticed before. He drew close enough for her to feel hot breath on her face. She cleared her throat and started to step back, but he held tight.

Tugging her closer, he hesitated, still mere inches from her face. Finally, he pulled her as close as he could and whispered in her ear, "Barbara, you'd do well to keep your distance."

"But you should—"

"Stop." Looking her in the eye, he reached up, held her jaw between his thumb and forefinger. "Your opinions aren't wanted by me, not now, not ever. I don't really care whether you wear pants, skirts or Eskimo parkas. You need to do whatever it is you came for and leave."

Barbara swallowed hard, tipped her nose up and jerked free of his grasp. She pictured a raging dragon blowing fire in her face, angry because the fair damsel was too strong. He couldn't gobble her up. With a slight shake of her head, she glared into his eyes.

Her jaw clamped together so tightly she could barely speak, but she did. "You don't frighten me, Jackson." *Oh, yes, you do. So much so, I can't believe I'm still standing.* "I don't begin to understand what happened to you, but wallowing in self-pity won't heal your scars. I'm sorry I ever met you."

He lifted his hand again, ran his thumb along her cheek. So gently this time she could feel the ridges of the troubled skin of his thumb. "So am I, Barbara. So...am...I." He reentered his room and closed the door. Once again, very softly.

Anger bubbling to the surface, her teeth chattered.

Father, I'm sorry for losing my temper, but he just doesn't understand. Burns and bruises don't make the man. You do. Please, wrap him in Your arms. Show him Your love.

Love? She thought the word, and her heart spoke it into being.

Barbara returned to her room and looked out the window while she brushed at the dark gabardine pants, dusting off the harsh words she'd said. This meanness of spirit wasn't like her. Well, he deserved to hear the truth. Now, she'd put her same forceful effort into helping Will and Mr. Judge. Make herself useful. And looking through her window, she could see that Will's efforts were downright pitiful.

Muscles twitching from her intense emotions, she banged through the house like a grizzly searching for his dinner and dashed out the back door. Heading toward the men in the yard, she screeched to a halt, her feet digging into loose ground. She had to calm down.

A little more charity.

The men looked up, went right back to work. Mr. Judge grunted while he nailed a long two-by-four into place. Will was working on one of the beams. But the gentle slant from the top to the edge didn't slope right. If only he'd adjust the angle slightly.

"It's no use, Dad. I don't work as well as Jack with my hands. I hate letting you down."

His father clapped him on the shoulder. "You're doing a fine job, son. With a few licks of the sander, we'll have this slick and polished."

She stepped forward. "May I help?"

He smiled at Barbara. "Hello there, young lady. My, don't you look the picture of fashion. Betty has begged for a pair of those silly pants for over a year. I s'pose we'll have to give in sooner or later and buy her some or we'll never hear the end of it." His face clouded. "Well I guess her beau'll be buying them for her, won't he?" His eyes took on a distant expression. "Still can't believe my little girl's getting married in three weeks."

Barbara shaded her eyes from the sun and looked up at the window to Jackson's room. Was it her imagination or did the curtains move? If only he'd join them. "Here, Will. I can hold while you sand. Tilt the sandpaper block like this."

"Hey, thanks, Miss Richardson—"

"You'd better call me Barbara."

"Okay. You sure are good at this. Who would have thought a girl could do carpentry."

"I used to help my father a lot when I was younger. After all, he didn't have any sons. Now, Mama says it isn't becoming for a girl to do that sort of thing. And I miss it. I was good at woodworking." She took one end of the two-by-four. "Here we go. I'll support the board so you can angle it just right."

Will struggled at first, the block flipping over the edge of the board, but then, after she had shown him a couple more tricks, he seemed to get the hang of sanding. "Hey, this isn't so tough after all. Thanks. But I'm not about to admit a girl helped me."

Barbara smiled and finger-locked her lips. "Our little secret."

From the corner of her eye, she noticed the curtain flutter again.

Chapter 6

Barbara giggled as Mrs. Judge divulged the last-minute details of her ruse to get Betty to her surprise shower. Mary Anne, Betty's cousin, had delayed the party so Barbara could attend. And late April had favored them with perfect warm weather, ideal for a garden party.

"Do you think she's suspicious?" Barbara asked when she cornered Mrs. Judge in the kitchen.

Betty's mother shook her head. "Not a bit."

They moved to the parlor where Betty folded half a bolt of material.

Unusually downcast, Betty plunked into the parlor chair. "Mother. Any reason why we have to take this fabric to Aunt Jenny tonight? Couldn't we wait 'til morning? I'm really tired."

Her mother reached for her arm, gently lifting her to her feet. "Young lady. Your aunt needs to finish Barbara's dress, now, doesn't she? She has the bodice finished, but she needs the rest of this fabric to finish the skirt."

Barbara wanted to laugh out loud at the story.

Betty's face lit like a firefly at the mention of her wedding, doing away with her exhaustion or blues or whatever her problem was.

Maybe Barbara would feel the same joy one day.

Two blocks over on Pennyman Lane, the three women stepped from Mrs. Judge's yellow Studebaker. Betty bobbed her head to the side, indicating the many cars parked next door. "Sure looks like their neighbors are having a party."

Her mother took notice and nodded. "It does, now, doesn't it? Maybe someone's birthday." She took a couple more steps. "Yes, I do believe I hear someone singing 'Happy Birthday.'" Then she hustled Betty through the yard.

Barbara choked back a laugh. She tugged Betty's arm against her, and they bounced up the steps, past forsythia bushes already blooming bright yellow. Betty knocked.

"The house is dark, Mother. Maybe they were invited to the party next door. We should have called first."

As Betty turned to go, her cousin, Mary Anne, answered the knock, a sheepish grin covering her face like Little Bo Peep. A dozen or more ladies, young and old, pushed into the entrance crying, "Surprise!"

Betty's eyes and mouth circled round with wonder. "For me?"

Barbara stepped back and giggled. "No, silly. For the Queen of Sheba. Who else but for you?" She hustled Betty through the doorway where more women waited, smiles wide.

A lace-covered table laden with sweet tea, pink ice cream punch, tea cakes, butter cookies and tiny finger sandwiches greeted them as they were escorted to the chairs outside. White paper bells interlaced with garlands festooned the grape arbor like a soft, white canopy. Gifts large and small dotted a card table, covered with a round bleached-muslin cloth that allowed the bright packages to shine against the plain white surface.

Betty hauled Barbara closer. "Everyone, c'mere. This is Barbara, my best friend from Indiana. You've heard me talk about her."

Barbara extended a hand, but hugs won out.

After cups of punch and most of the tea cakes had been eaten, Barbara parked herself next to Betty, collecting bows and paper. "Just remember, don't break the bows or you'll have to keep adding extra bedrooms onto your house."

"We don't have a house." Pink inched up Betty's cheeks. "But I'll be careful."

Her aunt's German neighbor, Anna Schroeder, scowled when Betty opened a box that held a feather tick and two feather pillows. "How beautiful."

The scowl turned into a huge grin. "You like dem? You use dem, right? You ladies still use fedders on your beds?"

Betty blinked back tears.

Barbara smoothed and folded the bright paper wrapping to use later as she admired the lovely plump pillows. She hadn't seen a feather tick since the one on her grandmother's rope bed. So comfy that when she and her sisters plunged into Grandma's bed at night, they got lost in the thick, marshmallow softness.

"Oh, Mrs. Schroeder." Betty sighed, taking the old woman's hands. "They're wonderful. We'll enjoy these forever." She patted the kind old hands.

Dusk settled like a blanket of semidarkness over the street. Jackson could still see out the front hallway window. His father struggled to unload the Studey all by himself. Jackson should be helping.

But if he did, he'd have to face her. He couldn't.

After another look at the pile of gifts, he realized how happy he was for his sister. Happy for his friend Teddy. Jackson only wished…well, wishing did no good unless you were five years old and blowing out candles.

Ships were sinking, chunks of metal propelled through the air in all directions from another blast and then another. He wished the Japs would turn back before causing any more deaths. He prayed he'd be able to save his friend Ollie. But the metal shaft from the ship's belly sliced across Jackson's face, then cracked Ollie in the skull, sending him into the dark, smoldering water. Churning fuel and debris closed over the surface like a coffin lid.

Jackson pivoted on his heel, leaving his father's struggles to sink along with his own memories. He sprawled across the bed and fell onto the soft pillow, arms over his forehead. How he longed to play a bigger role in Betty's celebration. If only he didn't resemble a gargoyle.

God, why did You bring her here? I could accept never having a wife, but to be forced to see her every day… It's not fair. To know she's just outside my door…sleeping feet from my room. Why are You torturing me this way? Didn't You do enough to me at Pearl Harbor? You could have saved all of us, but You let so many die. Why? Why didn't You at least save him? Jackson let the first tear since Pearl Harbor trickle over his scarred cheek and onto the pillow.

He swiped the tear away. Pity served no purpose. He waited for the noise to fade downstairs, put on his work boots and headed for the stairs.

There was work to be done.

Barbara tossed and turned on her bed. This was as good a time as any, though an excuse to talk with Jackson would help. She crawled out from under the covers.

Quietly, so as not to awaken Betty, she slid into slacks and a sweater. She strode to the cedar chest and picked out the delicate linens her sisters had made for Betty. A little after midnight, down the stairs and across the entranceway to the kitchen, she slipped on cat-quiet feet. With pillow-cases tucked under her arm, she pushed the door open. He needed a dose of reality. She was the woman to provide it.

No tall figure was perched on a kitchen chair sipping coffee and sulking. She glanced toward the back door. Cracked open. A moment's uncertainty developed into determination. Barbara walked outside and into the backyard where Jackson was sanding the gazebo; gentle strokes with his hands smoothed the boards to a satiny finish. She hesitated, listening. The cicadas' buzz competed with the soft grinding of sandpaper and stars glittered over her head.

Jackson stopped sanding, but didn't turn. "What do you want, Barbara?"

She cocked her head. "How did you know it was me?"

He tensed sweat-soaked shoulders so tightly under his cotton shirt, she could see the well-defined muscles. A wrenching sigh followed. "I can feel when you're near me."

Barbara sucked back air, pulled her bottom lip in as her heart skittered.

He returned to the long steady strokes with the rough paper. Even in the poorly lit area, she could see how nicely the gazebo was coming along. "Beautiful."

"Yes." His head sagged, but just for a second. "Very beautiful." Then he bent low, eyeballing one end of the board.

"I thought you might like to see one of Betty's gifts. My sisters sewed these for her." She held out her hands draped in the dainty linens.

He turned slightly. Barbara thought she saw a shudder before he returned to his task.

His deep voice spoke soft and low. "I'm sure Bets appreciates their hard work."

Her face flamed. The air stilled. Even the cicadas quieted as if sensing her anger. He cared for no one but himself, and it was time someone told him how it really was. "It's a shame you can't be bothered to look at these."

"Barbara, what do you want from me?"

What *did* she want from him? Certainly not this. Being treated as if she didn't exist. "You really don't care about anyone but yourself, do you? One of the most important days in your sister's life and you can't be inconvenienced to admire two of her presents. I can't, for the life of me, understand the mean-spirited selfishness you cling to as if it were your god." She dug a toe in the ground, welcoming the jolting pain.

Once again, his back to her, he stopped working. "Barbara, you shouldn't have come. My family accepts that I don't want to be around anyone. They just pretend I'm still away. That works for all of us. But you." He slammed the sanding block against the board and spun to face her. "You come here and expect things from me, things a man should be able to give a woman. That's more than I have in me."

"I *expected* you to have lost a great deal, but not your manners. No matter how hard I try to believe in you, you aren't the man my family met a year and half ago."

"I didn't ask you to believe in me."

Barbara yawned, pulled the quilt over her head. "Betty. Stop those bells. Aren't they louder than usual this morning?" When she poked her head out, they both laughed at the absurd question.

"You don't have to go to church if you'd rather stay here and sleep in. But you'll scandalize the whole town. At least the folks in New Hope." Betty, already dressed

and arranging her curls into wavy sausages on her forehead, gestured toward the clock. "If you are going though,
you'd best hurry. We leave in half an hour." She checked
the clock once more. "A short half an hour."

Barbara sat up, stretched, reached for her robe. "You
couldn't keep me here. I'm anxious to meet all the people who were so kind that Christmas. I figure most of the
town had a hand in the presents we received. We still talk
about our Secret Santas."

Blotting her red lips on a tissue, Betty smiled at her
through the mirror. "Oh, you think so, do you?"

"Secret or not, I'm sure I'm right about who the combs
were from, and I've never thanked you properly, Betty. I
use them on special occasions. I had actually planned to
wear them in my hair for my wedding, but we know how
that worked out."

"The combs...from me?" Betty stopped primping in the
mirror, turned and stared at Barbara, eyes wide enough to
pop. "Oh, no. I'm not so ritzy as all that."

"Then who, your parents?" Barbara rose and crossed
the floor.

"Are you kidding?" Betty asked. "I thought you knew."

Barbara rubbed sleep from her eyes as if seeing better
would give her a hint. "Knew what?"

"The combs were from Jackson."

Sun fought through the stained-glass window in the
front of the church where a beautiful carved cross appeared, rays shooting from each end. There was a strange,
uncanny peace surrounding her this morning, filling her
with hope. Church always did that to Barbara, but today
was different. She bowed her head when the families
prayed for their loved ones.

Father, I know You love Jackson. Please help him. He

*needs a reason to live again, to hope. I know it's easy for
me to tell him to stop feeling sorry for himself. I wasn't
there when he lost his friends, but I'm here now and I want
to help. Shove him out of bed so he can start living again.*

Barbara was so caught up in prayer that when the choir
started, she jerked upright. Betty cracked a smile. She
probably thought Barbara had fallen asleep. Not for a second. Listening to the words reminded her that no matter
how difficult the situation, He walked with her, spoke
to her heart, held her in His loving arms. An ache shot
through her heart when she thought of Jackson. He didn't
seem to believe in anything anymore. How empty he must
be.

Greeters pumped her hand on the way out and welcomed her back to New Hope.

A plump lady in a huge orange-flowered hat crowed,
"Elizabeth has talked about nothing but you coming to
visit. Welcome back to New Hope, child. We're happy to
have you here."

Barbara's head spun at all the good wishes heaped on
her. And she knew in her heart that Jackson would receive
the same welcome if he allowed these good people the
chance to show him. These weren't phony, fair-weather
friends.

With the day so bright and warm, she and Betty decided
to forego the car and walk home from church. Barbara's
stomach growled and that brought laughter to their lips.

Betty lifted her face to the sun, her cheeks like round
lady apples. "You should have crawled out of bed earlier
and walked with me in the garden. So much is blooming
now just in time for the wedding." She peeked at Barbara
from the corner of her eye and offered a calculating smile.
"But I s'pose you were tired, being out so late and all."

"You knew I was outside last night?"

Betty laughed. "You're about as subtle as a freight train roaring into the station. And not much quieter. Did you penetrate Jackson's thick skull?"

Barbara shook her head, powerless to stop the defeated expression she felt covering her face. "Not a bit." She wished she could say yes. "Jackson isn't blaming the Japanese or the navy for what happened to him. He's blaming himself. And God."

Betty breathed out a sigh from somewhere deep inside. "Time will tell."

Another rumble from Barbara's stomach reminded them they ought to hurry home to help with the meal. She pictured Mrs. Judge climbing out of the car and into an apron.

"C'mon. We'll be late and Mother needs all the help she can get. Besides, Teddy's supposed to arrive with his brother today." As soon as the words left her mouth, she blushed almost as red as her blouse and quickly shifted gears. "I'll race you home."

Barbara hoisted her skirt, pumped her arms and ran as fast as her legs would carry her, passing Betty easily.

Jackson peered around the edge of the hallway window, one of his favorite spots to observe the world racing by. Barbara's hair had loosened and heaped onto her shoulders in thick masses of soft brown curls. Her hair had been straight as a level and almost to her waist when they had first visited, but not now. Now it was curly, thick and shoulder length. His hand tightened on the window frame until it trembled. If only he could touch her hair, smell the fresh scent of shampoo he'd noticed that night in the kitchen. He shook his head; he had no right to touch her. No right at all.

Betty squealed and laughed as she and Barbara sprinted

to the doorway. What a tomboy Barbara was. He liked a girl with a hearty appetite for life. And plenty of spunk.

Had liked that kind of girl. Now, he didn't care. Not at all.

Truth lured him away from his watching place. Who was he fooling? He cared all right. Cared so much he actually thought about joining the family for dinner for the first time since he'd returned from Pearl. Hurting his sister and stealing her joy at a time when she should abandon herself to the wedding celebrations didn't sit well inside. Only he could change the circumstances.

Jackson crossed the floor of his room where a long look in the mirror stood witness to how far he'd fallen. That couldn't be him. Without sprucing up, he'd scare his worst enemy. Not that all the scars and burns could be covered, but at least he should clean up. He ran his tongue along the rough edge of his lip where the chunk of metal had sliced soft tissue. Couldn't very well walk around with his tongue over his lip. Like it or not—and he didn't—the red scar had to show.

His clothes hung in the closet, pressed, starched, neat and crisp as the day his mother had hung them there. But he stayed in Levi's and flannel shirts all the time. Even his boots had muddy clumps on them from his working in the backyard at night. The gazebo was shaping up nicely. But time had passed to step up and really help Father. For this to come together in less than three weeks, Father and Will would need Jackson's assistance around the clock.

With a close shave and clean clothes, he braved a step toward the door. The pants slopped at the waist. How much weight had he lost these last couple months living on disappointment and coffee?

The door squeaked when he opened it. The sounds and smells of kitchen-work-in-progress grew stronger with each step toward the stairs. Would Barbara be in the kitchen helping Mother and Betty? He stopped and ran tense fingers through his hair.

Coward. You can do this.

He dared the inner voices to taunt him again. One step. Then another. Finally at the stairwell, he gazed down. Betty stood at the bottom, her jaw nearly unhinged.

"Jack? Is that you?"

The first wooden riser didn't announce him, but that second rascal squeaked for the entire household to hear. He halted. Betty shrieked, "Jackson's here. C'mon, everybody." No sense hesitating any longer.

Barbara poked her head around the corner just as his foot found the bottom stair. A cautious smile tipped the edges of her lips. "Well, look who's returned to the land of the living. I've been here an entire week and you never came to welcome me."

He rubbed his jaw where bristles had been. "We talked."

"You call that a welcome? *This* is a welcome."

She moved forward on soft, fluid legs; he couldn't steal his gaze away. Her skirt ended below her knee in a swirl of color that looked like a peach from Father's grove. No pant legs to obstruct the view this time. His glance rose to hers, and like the shining blue marbles he'd played with as a kid, her eyes invited him closer. Slender arms reached out and enclosed him in a hug. Her surprising strength sent shudders through his body. Towering above her, his chin came to the top of her head. She smelled so good. His arms twitched to keep from wrapping her up like a knot. But restraint lasted only so long. He pulled her to him.

"There now, much more of a welcome," she said, her voice barely above a whisper.

What was he doing? He let go faster than if she'd been fire. His arms tingled where she'd hugged him to her. And that clean, soapy smell in her hair left him weak and exposed.

She looked up at him, grinning—breathless with the same self-assured grace he'd fallen in love with that first day when she had glared at him through the car window, almost daring him to be fresh. That was a long time ago when he had had something to offer a woman.

"Well, don't you have anything to say?"

Words filled his throat but a lump stuck halfway, wouldn't budge. His family stared. Finally a croak pressed through dry lips. "Welcome, Barbara." He shifted his face away, as he had learned to do to keep people from seeing the worst of his scars, but her gentle hands reached up, took his face in her palms and turned him to look at her.

"Thank you. I had hoped to be welcomed by you." She giggled. "Now, I'm afraid all this hospitality has left me famished. I don't mean to be rude, Mrs. Judge—" she glanced her direction "—but I lollygagged so long this morning, I missed breakfast. I can't wait to taste that heavenly roast I've been smelling in the kitchen since we came home." Her hands stayed on Jackson's cheeks.

His mother tidied the edge of her apron and blushed, tears in her eyes. "Soup's on! Let's go, Will. Hurry along, all, we've got a starving waif in our midst." Her plump hands pulled Barbara to her, away from Jackson.

Barbara glanced over her shoulder and winked in his direction. His mouth opened and closed, wordless.

Chapter 7

Sitting in his chair for the first time since he'd left for boot camp, Jackson relished the way his muscles relaxed. He leaned against the seat back, crossed his legs at the ankle and bowed his head out of respect for his father when prayers started. Nothing like the rushed gobbling of food once they sat to eat on ship. There had been a sprinkling of prayers, but mostly hand-to-mouth wolfing down of the worst food anyone could imagine. Lots of Tabasco sauce had doused eggs, meat, sandwiches, soup; even an occasional dessert.

Jackson opened his eyes to enjoy the sight of his family sitting at the table. As he scanned the row to the left, he gulped. Barbara stared at him. She immediately dropped her gaze and finished praying.

Father ended just as the doorbell rang. Betty said, "Amen," and flew to the front of the house without excusing herself. "It's Teddy. It's Teddy. He's early." She stopped long enough to address her mother. "Can you put two more plates out and add a little water to the stew, Mother?" An embarrassed grin followed her out of the dining room.

Add a little water to the stew. He smiled, remembering Grand's expression.

If Jackson meant it about changes for his sister's sake, he'd be forced to go all the way. Playacting wasn't exactly his forte, but he'd do his best. A test of his endurance.

Ted entered, Betty tugging his arm. Jackson rose to shake hands. "Good to see you." No chance hiding the scars. "Where's Teo? I heard he was coming with you."

"He'll be along in a couple days. He couldn't take so much time off work as I could. After all, I'm the groom. Who'd want to try and stop a groom?" He squeezed Betty to him unable to hide the love in his eyes.

A couple more days reprieve from the older brother; for that, Jackson was grateful.

Betty glanced toward Barbara. "This is my fiancé, Teddy. Actually, I'd like you to meet Theodore Barrymore the Third."

Barbara's eyebrows shot up. Impressed, was she? Wait 'til she heard the whole story. He surprised himself by repressing a chuckle.

Teddy leaned forward, pecked Barbara on the cheek, and said, "Nothing so ostentatious, I'm afraid. My father, for whatever reason, named my brother Theodore Jr. and apparently thought it would be clever to name me Theodore the Third. Rather gauche, but you have to know my father. So my brother goes by Teo. We had a great grandfather from France, and Teo thinks he's all French and swanky. But everyone calls me plain old Teddy." He slugged Jackson's shoulder. "Except the big guy here, who insists on calling me Ted. Trying to make me more manly no doubt."

He made a face and Jackson waited for Barbara's reaction. As he thought, she had a good laugh over Ted's antics. How he appreciated her sense of humor. Of course, in a few days, she'd have the real test. Teo Barrymore would arrive and then she could decide whether he really was everything he thought.

Barbara had every right to be enamored of the handsome, dashing Frenchman. In school, Jackson hadn't known one girl who didn't blush when Teo passed by. Until they got to know his groping nature better.

An hour later, when coffee accompanied big wedges of shoofly pies, Jackson hadn't offered much in the line of conversation. It had been so long since he'd interacted with anyone, words eluded him. After the last bite of pie, he excused himself, changed into his favorite old work shirt and headed for the backyard.

Mom called from the mudroom. "Not on Sunday, Jackson. It's the Lord's day."

He stepped back in and dropped a kiss on her cheek. "The Lord won't mind if I help with my sister's wedding."

Father walked around his mother and joined him. Hoisting some of the tools from Jackson's hands, he said, "And the Lord won't mind *me* helping my boy." He flashed a grin.

Teddy joined them, slapping Jackson on the back. "Don't leave me in a house full of women."

Jackson's mom patted Ted's cheek. "Not to worry, boy. We have to go for the final dress fitting. Don't you fellas work too hard."

Hair whipping every which way, Barbara dashed around the side of the house. Jackson grasped the hammer tighter to keep from dropping it. Trapped breath held his throat captive. He couldn't look away.

Her cheeks glowed and her eyes sparkled with life. Confidence brought out all her inner beauty. Twelve-penny nails were pressed between his lips. He couldn't smile, but for the first time in a long while, he wanted to. Wanted to smile, pull her close and tell her exactly how she made him feel. Maybe in time.

Or maybe not.

His father, in a long sweeping motion, chucked a piece of wood his way, grabbing his attention. "Lovely, isn't she?" But Jackson turned away, desperate not to choke on the nails.

"Hmm?"

Father laughed. "You know who I'm talking about. Don't try and fool me."

Barbara dashed to Jackson's side, poked him in the arm and ran her fingers along the pillar nearest his shoulder.

His father grinned.

With a sigh as light as a spider's web, she said, "Jackson, this is so smooth. Like a stone from years in the water. You do marvelous work. Why did you spend all those years in a hot factory? You should have been building cabinets or furniture…or gazebos. When will it be finished?" She nudged his arm. "Do you think there's any chance you'll have it done tomorrow?"

He spit the nails into his palm and set the saw blade aside. "Slow down." Then he pulled her fingers away from the boards, wanting to kiss them one at a time until she closed her eyes and…no. Even closing her eyes, she'd be able to picture what he looked like.

"What's wrong?" Her face fell. "Did I say something wrong?" The sad look pleaded with him to open up, tell her about his pain, but he couldn't. Wouldn't. "Oh, Jack. What's the matter now?"

The frown overtook him until the muscles in his head pulled tighter than a band. "You should go in. Help my mother. She's got a crowd to feed and you know she likes your company."

"What about you, Jackson? Don't you like my company?"

He looked around, helpless. His father's eyebrows shot up as if to say, *Go ahead, son, and tell her how you feel.*

Jackson plucked up the hammer again, grabbed the nails and pushed her toward the house so he could resume the job. Work relieved the tension, let him feel like a man.

Her feet tripped over themselves as she rushed to get away, but he had to keep his mind on task.

"You all right, son?" His father's face expressed a kaleidoscope of worry. "Why don't you go in and see what sidetracked Ted. Maybe get us a drink of water?"

Jackson shook his head. "Supper will be ready soon enough. Better we stay out of the kitchen."

Air hissed through Father's teeth. "Can't say as I agree with your lack of gumption."

Feelings hurt and bruised, Barbara rushed into the house. She offered her help to Mrs. Judge. That way Betty could sit on the porch with Teddy, enjoying the warmth of the late afternoon sun and the sweet smell of honeysuckle. According to Mrs. Judge, the bushes had bloomed early this year. The whole season seemed warmer than usual. New Castle hadn't experienced an early spring like this. So she welcomed the warmth.

"Let me run up and change into work clothes. I'll be ready to help in two shakes."

"Of a lamb's tail." Mrs. Judge laughed. "Take your time, dear."

As Barbara walked toward the stairs, she glanced out the window to the porch and noticed the two lovers head to head, undoubtedly heart to heart.

How lucky for Betty to have found a man so grounded, so full of life. And so in love with her. If only…but *onlys* didn't count. She sprinted up to her room and quickly changed, then hiked back to the kitchen.

"Can I cut the biscuits for you?" Barbara drifted to Mrs. Judge's side and took the cutter from her hands. "You've done enough today. You should rest." She dipped the cutter in flour. "I don't believe I've ever seen you sitting down."

"Oh, fiddlesticks." She hugged Barbara to her. "I'm just getting started, young lady. But you're more than welcome to cut those biscuits. Just make sure they're good and thick, all right? Can't tolerate scrawny biscuits on my table. They have to be hardy to hold all the applesauce and honey."

As Barbara cut into the light dough, piling piece after piece on the heavy metal cookie sheet, she heard feet stomping and loud laughter from the front room. That couldn't be Jackson; sounded more like Teddy's voice— almost. But it wasn't Teddy, she was sure.

Within seconds, a stranger entered the kitchen, but this man had Teddy's face or as close as two faces could be.

The man dashed to her side, lifted a clean dish towel from the counter and touched it to her nose, startling her. "You've a dot of flour on your nose." After which he bowed elegantly and reached for her hand. "Allow me to introduce myself. I am Teo Barrymore—Junior. And you must be the infamous Barbara Richardson from Indiana. The whole family's heard tales."

Her face warmed. My, he was good-looking. "Good ones, I hope." She set the cutter down, wiped her hand on her apron and offered it.

"Always." He ignored her hand, clipped her under the chin and slumped into the chair nearest her. "I don't s'pose there are bad tales to tell, you're much too pretty to have drama following you about like some Shakespearean tragedy."

His legs crossed at the ankle in a manner that suggested he was very comfortable in the Judges' house. He must be a frequent guest.

Handsome, regally handsome. No wonder he called himself Teo. He looked like a Teo: eyes worried with heavy lids and long lashes, a firm mouth carved from granite, hair far too long for a man of this day and age, but so alluring. And his nails had been recently manicured. Teddy didn't seem to be from money. Didn't put on airs at all, but this man oozed high society. He might be quite a catch if given half the chance. Unless he was all air, like a salty piece of chocolate-covered seafoam candy.

"I thought you weren't arriving for a few more days, Mr. Barrymore."

"Oh, my boss is a good egg, Barbara. He decided to let me leave not an hour after Teddy called. So, I hitched the royal team to my wagon and here I am. Now I'm glad I decided to come early."

What might the royal wagon mean? A pricey, showy car no doubt. "I'm sure Teddy's glad you're here."

"Only has eyes for his ladylove." He stood to his feet, landing right beside her. "Speaking of love, I understand you'll be my partner at the wedding." He looked to Mrs. Judge. "Isn't that so?" He dwarfed Barbara's hands in his. "I always appreciate a stunning face."

"You understand correctly, Mr. Barrymore." She blushed. "Not about the stunning face. I—I meant—"

"Teo, please."

Mrs. Judge busied herself at the sink without much to say. Did she like Teo or not? He did come on a bit, no, *quite* a bit strong—in a captivating sort of way. He was

Teddy's brother, after all, and Teddy was all goodness and amiability.

Barbara, a tad flustered by the rush of attention, indicated the cutting board. "Well, Teo, if you'll excuse me, I have biscuits to cut."

He stood behind, just inches away from her ear when he spoke over her shoulder. "Allow me. I'm an expert in the kitchen." He quickly washed his hands and nudging her aside, he grabbed the biscuit cutter.

Like an expert chef, he kneaded the dough and rolled it thick. With a flick of the cutter, snip, snip, snip. A dozen perfect biscuits ready for the oven.

Barbara nodded to Mrs. Judge. Pleasantly surprised at his ability, she laughed when the flour found its way onto his jacket. He was loud, boisterous and while not used to men like that, Barbara soon found herself caught up in his high jinks.

She shifted one of the biscuits for more room. "You surprise me. So adept in a kitchen."

Was she flirting with this man? Her mother wouldn't approve. But she was—she was flirting with a total stranger. "Are you always so charming, Mr. Barrymore?"

"Teo, remember? And yes, I work very hard at being charming. It's not easy, you know. Particularly around attractive women." He waited for a response.

"I'd say you're quite good at it."

After taking the first batch of biscuits golden brown from the oven, Mrs. Judge stepped forward. Barbara breathed in the fresh, delicious scent of bakery.

Betty's mother spoke in low tones to Barbara. "Could you call the rest of the family, dear? I'll be spooning up dinner in a minute. By the time they come to the table, this next batch will be done."

Teo glanced from Mrs. Judge back to Barbara. "That's

my cue to leave, I believe. Better get slicked up for dinner." He ran a hand through his thick hair. "See you later."

Barbara grinned, but didn't understand the sour expression overtaking Mrs. Judge.

With a groan, Jackson took in all the looks at the table when he arrived late, his clothes disheveled from hard work. He noticed a speck of sawdust stuck to his pocket and tried to swat it away without anyone seeing. Maybe changing for dinner should have been a priority. Not that it mattered. Now that the Frenchman had arrived, Jackson wouldn't be noticed if he wore sack cloth, a tuxedo, or what he was born in.

Teo glanced up. His face registered what Jackson feared when meeting people for the first time since his accident. "How goes it, Jack, old man?" He stared at Jackson, top to bottom and cleared his throat. "Good to see you up and around."

Jackson's mother clucked her tongue.

"I'm fine, Teo. Mom, let's eat. That leftover roast and biscuits sure smell good. Extra mashed potatoes. And gravy. All that hard work's made me hungry. Oh, and, Will, could you pass the milk? How about a scoop of applesauce for the biscuits." A rambling idiot added to the menu. Why didn't he simply shut up and eat?

Supper lasted longer than Moses' march out of Egypt. Jackson had hoped to retire early, but that wasn't to be. Barbara pulled him into the kitchen and draped a dish towel over his arm. "Thought you could help me. I told Betty to go for a walk with Teddy." She quirked a grin at him. "Poor Teddy's been shown all the wedding regalia and he probably wants to spend some quiet moments with his ladylove." She batted her eyes playfully.

Dishes? Sure. No problem. That's exactly what I want

to be doing next to you. And by all means, let's talk about love and couples finding time to be alone.

He pulled the towel off his arm and leaned against the counter. "She deserves a little happiness. If anyone has worked hard in her life, it's Betty. She started at Pennyworth's Five and Dime when she was just thirteen. Our parents have always encouraged ambition in each of us. And I think Betty's really done her part." *Babbling again. Shut up and dry.*

"There's a lot to be said for hard work." Barbara's face furrowed with what he recognized as her look of concentration. Perhaps memories of her own childhood aspirations. Maybe she was thinking of her dreams to be a singer.

"There is at that." *Say something clever. Tell her she's wonderful. Make a joke. Be a little more like Teo.*

She seemed to be waiting for a response, but when none came, she said, "I can see why you three men are such good friends."

He dried another cup and headed to the cupboard. "*Were* good friends." Now he'd done it.

"Why's that?" She snatched the towel and pushed him toward the sink. "Your turn to wash."

Jackson swallowed hard. Words cost him at a time like this when he preferred to remain silent. "Teo and I had a difference of opinion." He stopped. Any more was better left unsaid.

She smiled and brushed a curl from her cheek. "I'm sure if Betty and I were around each other every day, we'd have differences, too. Didn't you and Teddy attend Marion County's private school together?"

"We did." He dipped his hands in the hot water and a wave of nausea flooded his gut. After all this time, hot water still caused the pain in his hands to roar to life like a spark into flame, but he couldn't say so, or show any more weakness than he already had. He gritted his teeth as he pulled out a plate and rinsed the soap off. "Here you go. Yes, Teo was two years ahead of Ted and me. He… well, he liked to laud his status over us that he was the upperclassman."

Barbara blew a curl off her forehead and he saw the beginning of a frown. "Silly reason to hold a grudge."

"How about if we don't discuss Teo. That was a long time ago. We should concentrate on being happy for Betty."

He shouldn't bring up the past. Discussing Teo's bad behavior would only spoil the wedding for Betty and Ted. Barbara could go on guessing. What did he care?

"You don't like him then?"

"Give the girl a brass ring."

"Well, I was merely asking."

Was she hurt? She sounded hurt.

"You don't have to be grumpy."

"And you don't have to get snippy, Miss Richardson." He hauled bubble-covered hands from the water and punctuated the air under her nose with a finger. "I stopped getting lectures about my behavior a good five years ago, *Mom*."

"I'm not being snippy." Her face hardened as she choked the life out of the dish towel. "And I'm not trying to be your mother, Mr. Judge. The good Lord Himself can't bless her enough for raising an infuriating man like you."

"Then let's drop it."

"Fine with me."

Chapter 8

Waiting at the back kitchen door with a scarf over Betty's eyes, Barbara held her breath. Would Betty like it? The men had worked long hours to finish in time. When she had heard the whistle, she led Betty to the backyard where everyone stood around the gazebo. The sun faded fast behind them, giving them all an eerie, surreal appearance. All were present but Jackson.

"Take the scarf off. Please."

"Patience is a virtue." Barbara laughed and untied the knot in back. When she uncovered Betty's eyes, her friend defied her normal, excitable self: no hands clapping, no eyes sparkling, no lips pouring out words at an incredible speed. She stilled like Lot's wife, a pillar of salt, immoveable—and quiet. This was a different Betty altogether.

"Well?" Her father's voice quivered. "Do you like it or not? I can tell you right now, after all the hard work, you'd better."

Words came gently, uncharacteristically so. "It's lovely, don't you think, Teddy?" She looked his way, all the while running her hand over the wood.

Mrs. Judge's ideas sailed from her mouth like a grocery list. "And flowers trailing along here, a bit of netting over there in small clusters. Vines over this pillar and the pots of flowers I've been nursing in the greenhouse will fit here just fine, won't they?"

"I can't thank any of you enough." Betty looked past the hearty structure and took in the entire yard, her face a lovely combination of joy and speculation. "Where's Jack?" She gazed about. "I want to thank him."

Barbara's gaze drifted to the upstairs window.

When Will approached the dining room table, leaning in so all could hear, he did a silly drum roll with his lips. Barbara laughed until tears dampened her cheeks. She pulled a hankie from her pocket and dried the tears, but only momentarily. Will with his childish acting up had her laughing all over again.

Mr. Judge shook his head, straightened and took on the persona of a ringmaster. "Ladies and gentlemen, I would like to present—"

"Wait, Daddy. Jackson needs to be here. Please wait." Betty scurried from the room and Barbara heard her taking the stairs two at a time like her brothers.

In less than a minute she reappeared, cheeks pink and eyes filled with joy. "He's coming. Just wait a little, please." She turned to Barbara and spoke in confidence. "He had to slip out of his pajamas."

Teo tugged Barbara's sleeve and whispered in her ear, "Think we could do without him. He puts a damper on the whole party." She jerked her arm away and he frowned. "Well, he does."

Jackson appeared around the corner and she held her tongue.

"What's all the uproar, sis?"

Mr. Judge cleared his throat. "We'd like to present Theodore and Elizabeth with their first wedding gift." He tucked Mrs. Judge under his arm in what Barbara realized was a bittersweet moment for them. "This is an eventful day. A day we've all been—"

Mrs. Judge patted his cheek. "Oh, just give them the present, okay?" She was all smiles and her lips wouldn't be stilled. "Now you can do the drum sound, William."

His ears burned red. "Naw. Everybody's heard it already."

Barbara couldn't stop laughing. So much like her own family. Loving—good-natured.

Betty's father produced a long, thin box from behind his back. "What do you suppose we have here, dear girl? Maybe a toaster. Maybe a lamp, a very skinny lamp. Maybe a beautiful quilt handcrafted by your mother. Maybe a coat of arms from the family crest. Or maybe one box inside of another until you have nothing but a little package with tiny silver-plated napkin rings in the bottom. What could it be?" He chuckled at his jokes. "Don't give me that funny face, baby girl. Maybe we squeezed a million dollars into this box."

Betty hefted the gift with a little shake. "Awfully light for a million dollars." She dug in before her father could tease again. When the wrapping fell off, she pulled out a small card. After reading, she stopped, stared at her parents and grew quite still. "The card says…oh, I'm not sure I can do this without crying. Here, Father, would you?"

"Oh, no."

She put a hand on Barbara's arm. "Barbara?"

"Me? If it'll make you cry, my eyes will turn into Niagara Falls."

"You have to."

Going along with Mr. Judge's feigned formality, Barbara lifted the card from Betty's hand, straightened, cleared her throat and started. "It says: 'Your mother and I will be leaving the factory to your brothers as they have worked it since they were small boys. You helped, to be sure, but we thought we might show our appreciation in another way for you and Teddy. If you will take a drive along the back of our acreage, you will see a small clearing near the peach grove. By the end of summer, a four-bedroom cottage will be completed there for you and Teddy to raise your family. Please accept this as Mother's and my way of telling you how much you are loved and cherished. It is the last tangible thing we do for you as your parents, as your first family, before you and Ted become a new family unit. May God bless you and keep you both happy and strong in the years ahead. Your loving parents.'"

Teddy's mouth hung open and Betty clapped her hands. "Oh, can we go see it right now? Please?"

Mr. Judge waggled his mustache before twisting the ends. "You've seen that property a hundred times or more."

"Not since it was ours." Her eyes filled when she looked at Teddy, stars more than tears appearing there. "C'mon, Barbara. You and Jackson come, too. Pretty please?"

Barbara offered Jackson a look that entreated him to join in. "She's dragging out all the stops. What do you say?" If ever she tried to convince him to be sociable, this was it. Besides, there was something about Teo that made her uncomfortable.

Jackson waved a hand and shook his head. "No, sis. You go with Barbara. It's been a long day."

Barbara couldn't miss the way he eyed Teo.

"Okay," Betty said. "We'll drag Teo along. He's never seen the peach grove. And he's never too tired to have fun."

Jackson's eyes darkened, darker than Barbara had ever seen them. Better not add to what Betty already said.

Mr. Judge chuckled. "Wonderful idea. You kids run along."

Jackson heard them laughing when they came in around ten, stomping their feet at the back door. It didn't matter. He hadn't been able to sleep. Still trying to finish his new book, *The Ox-Bow Incident,* by Walter Van Tilburg Clark. He almost hadn't bought the western when he had seen the name and thought of VanDusen. Silly to think of that now.

Voices drew him to the door of his room.

Betty's call for reason. "Shh. We're too noisy. Mother and Father."

"Well, I'm not sleeping," Will chimed in, no attempt to lower his voice. "I got stuck taking the trash outside and burning it. Thanks for the mess, sis. That was one huge box for such a small note." Before long, he had joined them by the sound of it. They were all having a wonderful time. Without him.

What did he expect? He'd been invited; he had said no.

Jackson stuck his head outside the door. He should go downstairs and be sociable, but no, not with the Frenchman around.

Teo's voice carried loud and brash up the stairs along with the faint scent of Barbara's cologne. "Say, Betty. Isn't this where your mother hangs the mistletoe at Christmas? Will you look at that? Miss Richardson is directly under the spot. What do you say, Miss Richardson?"

Jackson's anger vaulted to the surface. His hand dug into his thigh.

"I'd say your imagination is working overtime, Mr. Barrymore."

Good for you, Barbara.

Betty's voice chirped with excitement. "How about a game of Monopoly? C'mon, Barbara. Let's get the box. We'll show you boys what for. Will, go grab some cookies and lemonade."

Teo spoke with no reserve. "I thought we had a more interesting game of Post Office starting right here. What say we send Junior to bed and have a go?"

Jackson started toward the stairs when he heard Barbara's voice raise a notch. "I guess that's one game you'll be playing by yourself, Teo."

Good girl. Sensible.

"I'm not much of a loner, Barbara. My tastes run more to boy-girl, boy-girl."

"I'm sure they do, but that little tidbit isn't going to get you anywhere with me. You need to settle down for a board game or leave."

The noise level quieted enough that Jackson decided he could sleep. Who was he kidding? He left the door cracked open so he'd be able to listen for any untoward complaints from the girls, and maybe catch a whiff of the flowery—lily of the valley?—cologne from time to time.

Each morning after breakfast, Barbara changed into her pants, rolled up her sleeves and forged ahead with preparations for the wedding, now closer than the women would have liked. Less than a week.

Mrs. Judge had engaged a woman from church to help get the baking done for the reception. Molly, according to Betty, was an Irish grandma who often hired out for parties, arriving early and staying late. Barbara had been short on patience most of her life, but Molly proved an endless well of endurance as days passed tying ribbons, clipping flowers and baking honey cakes and pies from last year's fruit canning.

So Barbara found herself this morning in the kitchen, as usual, working on her second pie crust. The delicious fruit mixes were finding their way into one succulent pie after another.

Molly reminded her, "Don't waste a speck. We haven't any extra shortening. We've borrowed all we can for this wedding. Thankfully, Mrs. Judge thought to buy extra before the rationing started this month."

"Will we have enough for all these desserts?"

"We'll make do. A little less sugar, a little more honey. Some applesauce in place of shortening." She leaned toward Barbara with a smirk on her face. "I know every trick there is, darlin'. Never you fear."

"I can tell. I never would have thought of making peanut brittle with honey. And it's so good!"

"That it is. If all else fails, the guests will fill up on good homemade peanut brittle." She laughed and started singing again, as she did most of the day.

Jackson struggled to place the last fifty-pound container outside the gazebo opening. "There, the last pot of flowers. Dad, do you suppose Bets will visit you folks often?"

"Us folks? You make it sound like you and Will won't live near. You boys have plans to skedaddle out of town?"

Jack dug into another smaller pot, lifting the plant and shaking it free of dirt. He'd loosen the roots and transplant it into one of the larger containers. "No, I just wondered if you thought she'd stay close to you and Mother."

"I figure she'll have to. She's only going to be half a mile away. Would be nice if one day all you children lived close enough that my grandchildren could play together in the yard between. Make forts like you youngsters did. Have snowball fights followed by big pans of chili and some of Mother's lemon meringue pie. Mmm. The outcome's almost worth getting pelted with an ice ball. Summers when you and Betty would come home soaking wet from the lake leaving puddles over your mother's freshly waxed floor. Jackson, those are memories that will be with me until they lay me to rest. And longer, if the Lord's willing."

Jackson slapped his father's back. "Don't plan on that nap too soon. I'd like to have you around for a while." He stopped. Thoughts nearly betrayed him.

A small rabbit skipped over the wooden floor of the gazebo, rose on its haunches, stared at them and dropped down but remained in the gazebo. Jack shooed it with the tip of his boot. His father joked about rabbit stew, and still the creature stayed, not trembling, not ready to bolt. Like Barbara. Even though Jack had pushed her away, she had stayed, small and helpless.

Helpless? She was anything but helpless. She was a tyrant. Attila the Hun out to have her own way no matter who tried to stop her. *Helpless my foot.*

"Get out of here." He ran at the rabbit, stomping his boots as he went. The creature skittered faster than a streak of lightning, only a small white tail left to flick its goodbye. He had to find a way to make Barbara run away, even if he scared her.

Barbara's nose twitched at the heavenly aroma of fresh cherry pie cooling on the metal rack. Molly passed on the water spray followed by sugar and glazed them with a honey wash instead until they were a deep golden brown. Barbara salivated, wanting to dig in right away, unladylike or not. "So you say we can eat this one? You're sure?"

Mrs. Judge gave her a look, nothing more. The same

expression her mother heaped on her and her sisters when they dared to disobey. "I meant at supper, of course."

Betty laughed at the exchange.

Barbara grinned at Mrs. Judge, dashed to her side and hugged her. "I'm not so much trouble here, am I?"

"Lands, girl. You're no trouble at all. We're enjoying every minute of your visit."

Teo crossed through the doorway and perched on the edge of the table. "You talking about food again? Keep that up and you'll be as big as my Aunt Lois." He drew a large circle in the air and chuckled.

"Shame on you," Barbara said.

He leaned over the pie, broke a corner of the mouthwatering crust and popped it between his lips. "Wonderful."

Mrs. Judge's brows furrowed, but he didn't get the hint. He picked another piece off the edge of the pie. She untied her apron, dropped it over the back of a chair and left a chilly air in the kitchen.

Betty scooted after her mother. A glance over her shoulder told Teo she wasn't very happy with her future brother-in-law. "Behave."

Teo turned an innocent glance at Barbara. "What has their bloomers all knotted?"

"What did you say?" Barbara shook her finger. "Teo, you have a very fresh mouth." She reached over and slapped his hand away from the pie.

He tipped forward and touched the end of her nose. "Your bloomers in a knot, too? Anybody ever tell you you're cute when you're angry?"

Before she realized what she was doing, she drew back her hand, but he caught it. Holding her fingers tight, he pulled them to his lips. "There's only one thing I'd like more than cherry pie."

She whipped her hand back. "Well, good luck with that!"

Sprinting for the stairs, the sound of his laughter drove her steps forward.

A hand reached out as she passed the upstairs landing. Jackson squeezed hard. "You look like a hornet that's got its stinger stuck. Would you like to tell me what happened downstairs?"

If she told, there would be trouble, and that might spoil the wedding. Maybe Teo had just been kidding around. "Nothing. I'm just tired. It's been a long day baking in a hot kitchen. How about you?"

"What about me?"

"Are the plants all in place? If you'd like, we could walk outside later and look at them."

He withdrew his grasp as if she'd scalded him. "I don't think so. Glad you're all right."

I'm not all right. You're making me crazy.

Chapter 9

Later that evening after his last bite of pie, Mr. Judge groaned with satisfaction. Barbara laughed. There was truth in the old saying about food being a way to a man's heart.

"Cherry pie. My favorite." He licked the edge of his fork and smiled. "Always has been my favorite. I could sit here all night until that tin is empty." He put down the fork, pushed back his sleeve and checked his watch. "But you young folks have been cooped up too long readying things for next weekend. Only five more days. I've never seen harder workers. How about a night out on me?" He reached for his wallet.

Barbara glanced from Betty to Jackson. What did a night out mean to Mr. Judge? Maybe that was a sneaky way of saying there were more chores this evening.

Will's face broke into a silly grin. He knew. "Anything special on your mind, Father?"

"I thought maybe a picture show followed by root beer sodas. My treat."

"You bet." Will jumped out of his chair, stared at the clock on the hutch, and shouted, "C'mon. We've only got half an hour before the first show starts. *Babes on Broadway.* Man, I really wanna see that. Mickey Rooney."

Betty leaned toward Barbara. "My brother, the movie aficionado."

Will turned, face creased. "The what?"

"Never you mind. Get washed if you're going with us. I'd *die* if anyone saw you with cherry pie on your chin."

"Aw. C'mon, sis. I washed before dinner."

She planted her foot, hands on hips. "You'd think you were still a child the way you behave."

He swiped at the red goo and started to wipe his hand on his pants. "I'm not a child and you know it." Only his tall stature belied the truth of her comment.

"William." Mrs. Judge leveled a look that said he might be missing more than the movie if he didn't straighten up.

Betty rolled her eyes. "And put on a clean shirt."

To Barbara's disappointment, Jackson excused himself and headed for the hallway behind Will.

"Not going, old man?" Teo leaned back in his chair to see around the corner. "We'll miss you."

"I'm sure."

Betty dashed to his side and whispered in his ear loud enough for Barbara to hear. "Please, Jackson. You know we'll have more fun if you go, too."

"I don't think so, Bets. Maybe next time." He pushed around her and strolled to the stairs.

"There won't be that many next times." Betty's face wore the hurt of a disappointed sister. "I'm getting married in a week."

Catching the look, Barbara stepped forward. "The movie's supposed to be a lot of fun. What do you say?"

She heard someone sneaking up behind her. Hands covered her shoulders and the culprit spoke up loud. "And I heard rumors Judy Garland's very fetching. Wouldn't want to miss seeing her fill the big screen now, would you?" Barbara stepped out of Teo's grasp.

Jackson turned, leveled a gaze until Teo backed away from Barbara.

Teo mumbled. "Only saying—"

She was grateful. Teo had no right to be pawing her.

"I know what you were saying. *And* implying. Good night all." He stopped and glared over his shoulder. "Ted? Be sure and take Will with you. Wouldn't want the kid to miss a night out with Barbara as his date."

Will balanced his bag of popcorn precariously in one hand. Teo did his best to slide past Will toward Barbara, but she held her ground. No way would she make room for the braggart next to her.

"And I graduated with honors at the University of Michigan. You should have seen the rest of the guys, pea green with envy. I ran the fastest mile, jumped the highest hurdles…"

Tuning him out was as easy as tuning a radio. One minute listening, the next so much static. Now here they were, Teo trying to make Will feel every bit the kid.

"I think I'll sit right here, Teo," she said.

"Just thought you might want to be seen with a man."

"Will is a man." She wrapped both arms around Will's elbow and glared at the screen. Then she peeked at Will out of the corner of her eye.

With his mouth full of popcorn, and a face redder than the wool seats, Will tried to speak. "W-whulph?"

"Hey, could you keep it down?" A man's deep voice shouted over Barbara's head. "Some of us wanna see the screen."

Teo slumped, spilling half his box of corn. "Never mind."

Relieved, Barbara smiled to herself, let go of poor Will's arm and relaxed. The popcorn was yummy, the picture *was* wonderful and Will's skin tone returned to a healthy hue. However, he moved as far to the other side of his seat as possible.

But the movie ended too soon. Heading toward the lobby, Betty and Barbara lagged behind the boys, commenting on each of the outfits Judy Garland had worn. Betty confessed she wished she could look like a movie star. "What a voice, and such a fashion plate. And her hair, it's always so perfect. Like she just stepped out of *Vogue*."

Teo shaped an imaginary hourglass with his hands. "That's not all that was so perfect, eh, Teddy?"

"Enough, Teo." Teddy wadded the paper sack into a ball and, taking aim, tossed it in the trash. "We have ladies with us."

Teo's head rose a step above the rest of them. "Man, you guys are about as much fun as the *Arizona*."

Barbara froze. Heat rushed up her neck all the way to her ears. "What was that?" Her hand flew up to stop him from answering. "Don't repeat it. I know exactly what you said." Her voice had risen sharply. "You're disgusting."

People stared. But Barbara didn't stop. "Didn't you pay attention when the newsreel played? Didn't you see the devastation from Pearl Harbor? We're at war. This isn't some game being played. I thought you a bit arrogant, but I never before believed you were truly cruel." She slapped his hand away. "Until now."

He grazed her elbow again and looked rightfully contrite. "Sorry, I didn't mean that the way it sounded." He gazed at the hostile faces around him and lowered his head.

"It strikes me as funny that you haven't enlisted, Teo. Healthy, strapping man like you."

His face paled. "I said I was sorry. What do you want?"

Barbara couldn't miss a snort and a huff from a man and woman not five feet away.

Some service boy's parents, no doubt.

Jackson's bed groaned under him. A feather pillow, the quilt he'd had since a child and a good book. He switched on the lamp. If only life could be as simple as a novel.

But it wasn't simple. Life meant dealing with people, accepting them and being accepted for who you were. He ached to have gone to the movies, Barbara on his arm, laughing, smiling at his stupid jokes. No way. The stares, the whispers, the steering around him in order to avoid conversation all played to his lack of confidence since returning from Pearl.

He punched his pillow and slouched against it.

His gaze drifted to the picture of the good shepherd on the wall. *Where were You when I cried out to You? You left us to drown. The frightening part is, I know You're real, God. That's what makes me so angry. You are real, but You deserted us when we needed You most. How could You have allowed that poor kid to die? He was a baby, only slightly older than Will. Why, God?*

Why didn't You save us? If only You'd saved Ollie. He didn't stand a chance. Like my own kid brother, Ollie barely grown up, and still You took him.

Noisy feet thundered over the floor downstairs.

"C'mon, Will. Let's see what's leftover."

Barbara's voice. The wedding party had returned. In his present state of antagonism, he figured joining them would make him the soaking-wet blanket. He unfolded on his bed, closed his eyes and pretended not to hear the laughter inviting him to play.

"I'll beat you to the kitchen," Will said.

Hungry because they hadn't stopped at the malt shop, Will and Barbara raced for the refreshments. Ted and Betty stayed behind on the porch, and Barbara didn't care one whit what Mr. Hotsy Totsy planned to do.

She marched to the refrigerator and poured tall glasses of milk for herself and Will while he cut small slices of the remaining cherry pie.

Now over the shyness he'd shown at the movies, he gazed over his shoulder, mischief his middle name. "Remember, Barbara, I get to kiss the cook if I find a pit."

Unable to stop the grin from spreading, she said, "Okey dokey." Then she leaned in close. "Just don't forget one important detail, son. Molly made that pie."

"Ugh." His face fell. "She's older than Methuselah."

"Be nice." Barbara chucked him under the chin, bringing a rosy-faced response that vaulted her smile to the surface again. "Say, how about you and I take these plates into the living room and play some Monopoly?" She glanced at the clock over the stove. "I'm getting my second wind."

Will pouted. "Didn't you beat me bad enough before?"

"No. I think with a little effort I could do a much better job of kicking your britches."

He loaded her with the tray of glasses and plates and strode directly to the cabinet that held the games. After rummaging a few seconds, he spun on his heel. "Think Jackson might be up to a game or two?"

His brother's name was no sooner out of his mouth, when he froze, not saying a word for the longest time. Slumping into a chair, he stared into Barbara's eyes, his face downright pathetic. A low moan accompanied the lip he'd tucked between his teeth. "Do you think Jackson will ever be himself again, Barbara?" He looked away, but she saw his fist pounding into the other hand.

She set down the tray and put an arm around his shoulder. "He has a lot on his mind, Will. None of us can know how terrible it was December 7. We can only guess at the horrors he experienced. I'm thinking it will take him as long as he needs to start to forget and to forgive."

"Forgive?"

"Yes, Will. In time, he'll have to learn to forgive the attackers. Forgiveness is the only way to move past the pain. And God's the one and only true way to do that. If we don't forgive, how can He forgive us?"

"As soon as I'm old enough, I plan to join up. I'll finish what Jack started!"

"Mrs. Judge, Jackson wasn't in his room. I knocked twice." Barbara awaited further instructions before plating the food for breakfast. If they didn't hurry, the eggs would grow cold.

Will entered and snatched a slice of bacon. "Don't wait breakfast on my big brother. He left two hours ago." The bacon crunched as he bit in. Talking with his mouth full, he added, "Up before the crack of dawn with a backpack full of food and a Thermos of water. Said he'd be gone a couple days. Not to worry, he'd be here before the wedding festivities started. Didn't he tell you, Mother?"

"He did not." Will's mother shoved fists against her waist. "And where was he going, pray tell?"

"Along the lake I expect. That's where he used to hike before…he went away."

Barbara laid a hand on Will's arm. "What does he do at the lake?"

"Camp, swim, eat, read, hike. I dunno. Just spends time where it's quiet. Nobody to bother him."

Barbara didn't understand Jackson. Probably wouldn't even if she lived to be as old as Mrs. Judge. "You'd think he would have had enough of being alone," she said.

Will's jaw twitched.

After breakfast, Barbara, Mrs. Judge and Betty sat at the table putting finishing touches on the scoops of netting that would be tied onto the gazebo. Barbara held a bouquet in front of her. "Well, do I make a beautiful bride?"

"You're going to be a very beautiful bride, Barbara." Bets snatched the netting clusters from her hand. "Someday. Maybe if Jackson—"

"Don't, Bets." Barbara meant to smile, but a combination of trembling lip and quivering chin overpowered her as she slumped back into the chair.

"You girls finish up here. I'll get started on the dishes." Mrs. Judge shook her head and walked from the room.

"I'm sorry." Betty put a hand on Barbara's arm. "I just thought. Well, never mind what I thought."

"Am I that transparent?"

"Sweetie, like a clean window after a squirt of ammonia. Ever seen little kids with their noses pressed to the glass at a candy store? My brother seems to be a creamy piece of divinity. And I've seen how he looks at you. All starry-eyed."

Barbara's arms hung limp at her sides. "You're reading too much into whatever you think you've seen. Jackson doesn't want anything to do with me."

"Oh, there you're wrong. You remember how Jack was. Confident, a little too much maybe, but still he knew his way around the ladies. Now, he perceives himself as some kind of creature that no woman would want. Don't you see that?"

Thoughts percolated and ideas bubbled to the top. One scheme that kept surfacing questioned how far she was willing to go to force Jackson's hand. How scandalous would it sound to the Judges? Jumping to her feet, she hugged Betty and ran from the room.

"Barbara?" But Barbara was already in the kitchen discussing her plan with Mrs. Judge.

Mrs. Judge turned from the sink, her face showing how flabbergasted she felt by the request. When Barbara asked if she could prepare a couple sandwiches, pack a bag and go find Jackson, the color had drained from the woman's cheeks like sand streaming from an hourglass. But amid Mrs. Judge's complaints, Barbara saw a flicker of hope in the tired eyes. As if she put stock in Barbara's ability to convince him to return home. Well, wasn't that what she was counting on—her finesse to encourage him to come back?

"All I can do is try," Barbara said.

Salt-and-pepper hair drooping in her face, Mrs. Judge pushed a curl from her forehead, the skin ruddy. "Now, you're sure your parents would allow you to go traipsing around the countryside if they were here?" She picked up a dish towel and wrung it in her hands as she spoke. Barbara thought if the towel were a chicken, they'd be having the poor thing with dumplings for dinner.

How could she say this and still be truthful? "Of course. We girls go hiking all the time when we're on the road with Father's work. I'll be fine." She had hiked that one time, years ago, when Mama's best friend had escorted them into the woods and back hunting for morel mushrooms. And she and her sisters had walked the woods whenever Father had worked near a wooded area. That was hiking, wasn't it?

"Very well then. You throw a bag together in case

it should rain—" they both knew it wasn't supposed to "—and I'll make you two roast beef sandwiches, toss in a couple sour pickles, apples and…"

She was still listing the menu when Barbara left to borrow a backpack from Will. Barbara wasn't even sure how to put one on, let alone hike with the weight.

A breeze blanketed the air along with the noisy crickets and grasshoppers. Water slapped the edges of the lake. Life should be so clear-cut. Each living his own way, minding his own business. People needed to learn the same rules as nature.

In his hand, an apple from last year's crop begged for Jack's attention and he bit in. Crisp. In no time at all, the orchard would be producing a fresh crop, continuing the cycle. Twelve peach trees, twelve apple, twelve cherry and five plum. Whatever happened to the other seven plum trees? He'd climbed them as a child. No matter. Plenty of trees survived to feed the family for a year and beyond. This apple represented hours of work, winter and summer. Spraying, pruning, culling the fruit so that each piece would be large and firm. Lots of work he and Will had done in the hot sun. He bit in.

Another bite. Sweet, like honey. Sweet—like Barbara. With a flick of his wrist, he threw the core and hit a rock, but juice continued down his chin.

Where did that thought come from? He was spending way too much time thinking about her. For what? No woman would look at him like he was a real man. A moan from deep within reminded him that none of that mattered.

He leaned over the edge of the lake and scooped icy water into his hands and over his face. Cold and refreshing. One more scoop and he was tempted to go in even though his mother's words echoed from childhood. *Can't swim in a lake until after the first of June.*

There was probably a good reason, but with the sun so unusually hot this time of year, the water called his name, enticing him to jump in. Maybe he'd float along the top for a few minutes and then take a nap. Checking to be sure he was alone, he stripped down to his shorts and stretched like a fat, lazy cat in a window box. So out of shape. Well, it didn't take a lot of stamina to float, or swim.

Once he started arm over arm, he couldn't stop. Kicking, pushing the water behind him, digging in, proving to himself he still had strength. In the deeper section now, he plunged beneath the frigid water, the air held low in his belly. Deeper and deeper he dove until he couldn't hold his breath any longer. This must have been how Ollie felt. Had he simply given up, pulled the tainted water into his lungs and willingly died? Or did he struggle, fight the water that rushed into his mouth, forcing him to breathe the fetid water-oil mix?

But they didn't mix. How was it that day they had? The oil and water and debris had turned into a swirling, angry pandemonium, choking the strongest swimmers in their unit.

Chest seizing, Jackson kicked to the surface, gasping for air. The swim to shore tested his muscles with burning pain. The shore seemed miles away. Jack's arms became heavy lead objects with each stroke. If he wanted, he could lean back, close his eyes and end his misery. No. Bets would surely cross from earth to the hereafter and rip him back for the wedding.

Now that brought a smile to his lips as he finished his swim to shore.

Chapter 10

He'd stretch out on the grass, listen to the water softly slapping the sand and sleep a while. Last night Jackson had done nothing but toss in bed after the wedding party had returned. He'd listened as long as he could tolerate Barbara's laughter. No doubt having a smashing time with Teo Barrymore. And why not? Handsome and rich as he— beautiful and intelligent as she. The perfect couple in every way. Together, Teddy and Betty, Teo and Barbara would be family and best friends forever. The thought turned his stomach bitter. In fact, the idea of Teo and any decent young lady drew acid to his throat until he strode back to the chilly water and drank enough to choke the burn down.

He knew better than to believe the phony show of good from Teo. Teo liked to love 'em and leave 'em. He'd made a career of breaking hearts at school and Jackson didn't have any reason to believe he'd changed.

Under the weeping willow that bordered the water, Jackson slid into his dry jeans and shirt and fell belly first onto the spring grass. Blue flowers—he couldn't think of their name—poked through, looking like…no! Uh-uh. Wasn't gonna do it. He flipped over and put the blue eyes out of his mind.

What had she been thinking? Barbara didn't know her way around the lake! Sure, the family had camped plenty when they had traveled with Father for his work. Father had built roads all over the country and she'd hiked some, but this was different. And the last time she had seen this body of water, it was in flood stage. She stopped and listened. Sounds wouldn't tell her whether or not she was going the right way. She didn't have survival skills. Didn't know what side of the tree the moss grew on or what that even meant. She wouldn't know a poisonous berry if she made jam out of it. How foolish to have come here alone.

She held a hand to her eyes to shelter them from the sun. The pack grew heavier, she grew hungrier, and the day grew longer. Soon she'd have to stop and nibble on one of the sandwiches jammed in the bottom of her bag.

This wasn't all her fault. Jackson's stubbornness had caused most of the problems she'd endured today. If he hadn't snuck away so early, she might have convinced him not to go at all. But that didn't seem likely. Jackson was the type of man to do exactly what he wanted.

Well, she was known to get what she wanted, as well.

Thinking back, she realized Jackson was one of the reasons she'd been so eager to break her engagement to Elliott. One of the reasons? He *was* the reason. Once he'd winked at her through the window, once she'd realized he wasn't the big flirt she had first thought, once he had smiled at her, she knew Elliott VanDusen didn't stand a chance. Elliott desired a beautiful wife to wine and dine his business partners. And to think, she'd nearly married him. Her desires had meant nothing to him.

She sighed, let out a breath so loud it startled a mallard bobbing on the lake. *Jackson, don't you know how crazy I am about you?* She watched the mallard as he skimmed over the water toward his mate. Even the stupid duck had a girlfriend.

Another hour and her feet hurt, her lungs burned from exertion, her skin tingled with sweat; she'd had enough hiking. Hands brushing against her pants, she took in the sand, rocks and trees just off the water, looking for a pretty spot to spread the shawl Mrs. Judge had tucked in. The sand looked too hot to sit comfortably. A shady place would be nice. That willow offered the best shade. And the ground was covered in wild violets. She opened her bag, drew out the shawl, and plopped against the tree. A sandwich would taste good right about now. She nibbled at the bread—tasteless. Pickle juice seeped out of the waxed paper and when she bit the end off, the juice trickled over her chin. There was a napkin in there somewhere. After dabbing at her face, she put the sandwich back. She wasn't that hungry after all. For now, she plucked a few of the violets and tasted their sweet mellowness.

Bark dug into her head as she leaned against the giant trunk. She'd close her eyes for a second. Soft lapping of the water filled her ears. Until...deep breathing startled her. An animal? She didn't see any. She crawled hand over hand and peered around the tree. A man slept on the other side. What had possessed her to come out here alone?

Barbara stood up—took a good look at the sleeping figure. Tall. Well-muscled shoulders strained against the fabric of his shirt. Dark hair, wavy. He almost looked like... Jackson? It *was* Jackson. Like Goldilocks, here he was.

Afraid to move for fear of awakening him, she tiptoed

around, then sat against the other side of the tree again. Her heart rate ratcheted, breaths coming rapid and shallow. If she thought he had frightened her before with his behavior, she was petrified now.

Untying her sweater from her waist, she dropped it on the ground and eyed her watch. Ten-thirty. She'd been walking for over three hours. The sweet smell of spring captured her. She breathed deeply of the fragrance, allowing the scent to calm her, wishing she could capture the aroma in a bottle to take home to Indiana when the time came. But more than just the smells of spring enticing her, Jackson's nearness fascinated her. She could look all she wanted without him jumping up and storming to his room. He couldn't stop her from staring, taking in his wounds.

Barbara gazed around the side of the tree for another peek. Jackson's hands. Strong, callused, a workman's hands. With his sleeves rolled to the elbow, and his hands crossed on his forehead, his scars were visible, vulnerable to her probing stare. At the house he'd been so careful to keep his arms covered and often wore work gloves. She imagined how hot the water must have been when he had reached in to save those men. At least he'd tried. Even though they didn't escape, he'd made the effort.

She cringed, remembering when she had told him it was his turn to wash dishes. And he had shoved his hands into the hot dishwater without complaint. *Way to go, Barbara.*

Her gaze traveled over his face. Thick black lashes lay above the swell of his cheeks. The jagged cut through his forehead peeked around his hand and still rose red against his skin. But it wasn't ugly. Oh, how she wished he could see himself the same she did.

God, I asked You to let Jackson see himself through Your eyes, through my eyes. Please, Father. He needs You

*now more than ever. You're the only chance he has for a
normal life.*

She lingered, staring another three or four minutes before inching closer. If only she were brave, she might move
right next to him. But in doing that, she wouldn't be able
to resist laying her head on his chest, listening to the beat
of his heart. Proof he'd survived Pearl Harbor.

Barbara sighed and leaned her head against the tree,
hoping for a drop of wisdom to seep from the gnarly aged
bark into her brain. What could she do to convince him
that he was more handsome than any other man she knew?
Had ever—would ever—know.

Willpower gone, she leaned to the side, glimpsing again
the fascinating face. How she longed to take his cheeks in
her hands and kiss each inch of that wonderful face until he
kissed her in return. *Really* kissed her. She sat back. Such a
thought. Heat swelled from her neck to the tips of her ears.

Mama would think she was worse than a floozy if she
dared kiss him while he slept. But Mama wasn't here. Jackson was. She pulled in her bottom lip, thinking. Should
she? Or would she regret the rash decision?

Palms resting on the soft grass, she edged forward. A
few minutes passed while she worked up the courage to
move even closer. She traced every line of his face, not
with her finger, but with her heart. So serene in sleep. No
anger. No hurt. No concerns about his appearance. She
longed to shake him and force him to realize how much
she meant to him, but that wasn't possible. He'd have to
discover those emotions on his own.

*Father, at some point, I have to let him know I love him,
or I could lose him forever. He means the world to me.*

Ever so gently, she bent down, placed one hand on the
ground and the other on his chest. Leaning in, she touched
her lips to his—warmed from the sun. Her eyes closed

of their own accord as she dreamed of him loving her as much as she loved him.

Whoosh! Air burst from her lungs as strong arms encircled her, crushed her to him, as she was kissed back.

Softness and warmth, tickling his lips. Errgh. Dreaming about Barbara again. Well, why not make the best of this dream? Jackson reached around before the dream could evaporate to wherever dreams go. He filled his arms with the only woman he'd ever loved, and he kissed her. Kissed her the way he'd wanted to since the first day he had seen her sitting in the car afraid for her life. Sweet lips clung to him, tasting of honeysuckle and wild violets in the spring. His arms forced the hallucination closer and closer. For a dream, she certainly felt real.

Oh, Jack. Don't ever wake up. You might not have her in life, but in your dreams, she is your Barbara and yours alone.

Heart pounding, he let the thrill of the moment surround him. If this was what his dreams were made of, he'd sleep forever.

Opening an eye, he froze—quickly closed it again.

Not a dream.

His arms tightened. Another look. Barbara? This wasn't happening. How? She was home with his family.

Okay, Jack. Your mind is playing terrible tricks. Cruel tricks. You're going to wake up any minute and she'll be gone. Like his sister's childhood story. Cinderella at midnight. Poof, in rags again, her coach a pumpkin.

This time, he'd open both his eyes and the phantom Barbara would have left along with his troubled sleep.

"Jackson. You're crushing me."

Illusions don't talk. "Barbara!"

"H-hi, Jack."

The crooked smile, filled with uncertainty, prevented him from shoving her away. But he untangled his arms and gently set her aside. Warmth crept from his neck over his face and settled in for a few moments of humiliation.

"What are you doing here?" He rose, rolling his sleeves down to cover his arms.

Her mouth hung open. For once, she didn't have much to say. "I—I…"

Brushing sand from his pants, giving him time to think, he said, "I asked you a question. What are you doing here?"

No longer did he care whether or not he hurt her feelings. She hadn't the right to be following him, checking up on him like he was a child.

She cleared her throat and blinked rapidly. "I—well, I came to find you."

"That's obvious." Anger quickly replaced his embarrassment as he seethed beneath the surface. Nipping the edge of his lip, he worked hard to keep his anger in check. "But what gives you the right?"

"Everyone was worried." She drew herself up from the ground.

"Everyone?"

"Yes, of course." She changed before his eyes. Sweet little kitten of a girl became a mama cat ready to pounce. "Everyone! You don't think *I* care one bit?"

Aah, good. The Barbara he knew, full of vim and vinegar, back in a blink.

"I came because your family was worried about you."

"My brother would have come if they were truly worried."

"Let's not argue—"

"Barbara, why can't you leave me alone?" He punched the tree. Whoa. The tree held its ground well. He lifted skinned knuckles to his mouth. "If I'd wanted you here,

I'd have asked you to come." He turned away from the look on her face. Hurt or anger? It killed him to be mean, but she had to understand. There couldn't be anything between them. "Barbara, I needed to be alone. I want to think. Sort things out, and I can't do that with you on my mind every second of every minute of every long day. Having you live under the same roof. Watching you smile and laugh. Seeing you…"

He looked back when he realized he'd said way too much. The hint of a smile edged her lips. She was winning.

Barbara took advantage of the time to sweep dirt from her clothes before she laid it all out in front of him, the truth, as she saw it. "So, I am on your mind. What was that? Every second of every day or something or other?"

"That's not what I meant." He struggled to say what was in his head instead of his heart. Barbara could fluster a diplomat. Give the army a squadron of women like her and the Japs would run for cover. She could make a grown man stutter and tremble like a little boy caught with his hands in the cookie jar. His wet, clammy hands. He wiped his damp palms on his Levi's . Worse yet, she knew who held his heart captive. She did.

His knuckles dug into his thighs until he welcomed the pain. "You're twisting my words."

"Sure I am." Her eyes connected with his and dared him to look away. "I will hike this lake, sit under a tree, or bathe in the water in my altogether if I so choose, Jackson Judge. You might have your family hoodwinked, but you don't fool me." She crossed her arms and leaned against the tree. "I…was on the other side…of that kiss."

"I don't know what you're talking about."

Her brow rose and her lips pursed in a line so straight a sergeant would have been proud. Then she smiled, not coy or cute or even smug, but wise-guy beautiful. "You know precisely what I'm talking about. And if you were the man I think you are, you'd admit you're in love with me and stop all this nonsense so our families could be as happy as we will be." She tapped her foot against the ground like a rabbit thumping. "Well? Are you or aren't you?"

What had she asked? "Aren't I what?"

"In love with me, Jackson."

"In love with *you*. What makes you think I'm in love with you?" Sweat punctuated his speech. His hands trembled at his sides while his gut slithered in circles.

She arched a brow, the intense blue eyes reading him. "Well?"

"Not on your life."

Her voice softened. "Oh, Jack. You *are* in love with me. A real man would just say the words and get it over with. 'I love you, Barbara, and I can't live without you.' It's not that hard to say. You don't need a Harvard law degree to put—" she stopped and counted on her fingers "—ten words together."

His hands fisted. *A real man*. If she said that again, he was going to punch something. Looking around for a likely target, he spied the tree again and mentally shook his head. If only Teo were here, then he'd punch something for sure.

But Barbara was right…on every count. No matter that he'd tried to spare her half a man. At least he was half a real man. Not a fop like Teo.

A *real man*. He'd show her. He had more of what it took to be a man in one of his scars than Barrymore had in his whole body.

Staring into her eyes, doing his best to read her thoughts, all he could think to say was, "You want a real man, huh?" Without another thought to the consequences, he grabbed her by the shoulders, wrenched her to him and kissed her—hard.

When he finally found the courage to open his eyes, hers met his, and they were brimming with compassion. "You *are* in love with me. Why won't you say it?" Her face radiated joy, but he couldn't say what he knew would hurt her in the end.

Damp curls plastered her skin. Her cheeks, rosy and sweet, beckoned him to kiss the petal softness again. He could feel his determination slipping away, one blue eye at a time.

But she deserved better. Why was it so hard for her to see that? He shoved her out of his arms. "Go away, Barbara."

"Jackson, don't do this."

He licked dry lips. She'd be hurt in the long run. Doing his best to free himself of her, he sucked back air. She deserved a VanDusen or a well-deserved singing career. Somehow, he would have to make her believe he didn't care.

His arms opened wide. "What do you want from me?"

She stepped closer; he stepped back. "I want you to love me, Jackson."

"Even if I wanted to—and I don't—I couldn't. I don't want anyone or anything. Only to be left alone."

"But you do love me. I can tell."

"You'd like to think that, but the truth is, you're not my type. Never have been." He leaned forward, pecked her lips like a big brother. "See? Nothing. Just a kiss to make you happy. That's all I've ever wanted. Like under the mistletoe, one more conquest. That's all you were, Barbara. I've always been attracted to what I can't have."

Shades of Teo filled his mind. Shudders ricocheted through him for the cruel comments. But this was for her own good. He did a complete turnaround and walked to the edge of the water, tears welling. "You'll find someone. There's the right man out there. It's just not me."

The apple he'd eaten rose in his throat and he swallowed, forcing the burn down. Noises thundered in his head, voices that told him to stop wishing.

Chapter 11

Stumbling back to the Judges' house, tears bathing her eyes, Barbara crumpled against a log blocking the path. She slipped the pack from her shoulders. Quiet mocked her as she sobbed against the back of her arm. He wasn't the man for her? Of course, he was. Surprised by his cruelty, she hiccuped a sob and switched from hurt to anger faster than Jackson could have said *I love you*...if he had had the nerve.

Her father hadn't raised a baby. He'd taught her to be strong. Sitting alone in the wild, nursing hurt feelings like a whiny brat didn't speak well of his instruction. "No matter what you want in life, Barbara, you can have it. You work hard, you make plans, and you go after whatever it is. Never say die."

Never say die.

Did that apply to relationships? She picked at a piece of bark on the log, contemplating her father's words. Well, why not? If she wanted Jackson badly enough, she would force him to admit he loved her.

Let's see how he'd like it if she *did* find another man. Maybe a taste of the green-eyed monster would persuade him to face the fact that he loved her.

A sudden barb in her heart questioned the plan.

Why not wait for God's timing?

She was. Only she'd make Jackson a little jealous to hurry things along.

Not by deceit.

She wasn't deceiving anyone, not really. Standing and brushing dirt from her slacks, her head swirled in what she recognized as justification for what she was about to do. Just playing a game. Like Monopoly or darts.

Kissing her one minute, hauling her so close a gnat wouldn't have been able to flit between them. Barely a second later explaining how she meant nothing to him. Real nice. Jackson wasn't kidding himself. When he had wrapped his arms around her, he'd escaped into the moment, hadn't intended to let go.

A man didn't get a hundred chances to make things right. And he had let his best opportunity for happiness walk out of his life. He fell to his knees near the water, submerging his legs.

Why, God? Please. All I want is to be left alone. Let me forget her smile, her eyes, her loving nature. Let me forget everything about her. I want to be alone! You know that. You know exactly what I want. Please help me.

Hiking had lost its appeal. Another leisurely nap under the willow tree would solve nothing. His head ached, muscles cramped and a tightness had crept across his shoulders and neck like a band of steel. He might as well go home.

* * *

Barbara stared at the huge white house, windows like eyes winking at her. She staggered to the porch, dropped her bag and collapsed in the swing, her feet pushing and relaxing, pushing and relaxing, just enough for the seat to sway gently. The squishy cushion and the soothing rhythm eased her pain, but not for long. Memories didn't die because a swing calmed a person; the mind continued its thoughts, darting from topic to topic. She snuggled against the big pillow that ran the length of the swing. If only the pillow were Jackson. She might cuddle up and stay there forever, safe and snug.

Daydreams. Only daydreams. She closed her eyes, but felt again the warm breath on her face just before he had kissed her. His lips, firm but gentle, had proved to her how much he loved her. The front door opened and a porch board creaked under a heavy foot. Jackson had returned.

"Who's the lonely lady and why are there tears in those lovely eyes?" Teo sat down, nudging her aside.

Barbara scooted over to make room for the Frenchman, but she would have preferred Jackson. "Memories. Some good, some bad. A few needing to let go once and for all. What did you do today, Teo? Something terribly amusing, I'll bet."

When he twisted a piece of her hair between his fingers, she caught the odor of cologne. Expensive cologne. "Sat around thinking of ways to cheer up a beautiful girl, why?"

She shook her head, felt the rush of heat in her cheeks. "Oh, you are the ladies' man, aren't you?"

"That hurts." He grinned and grabbed his chest.

"Teo, I doubt anything or anyone hurts you for long. I wish I had your carefree nature."

When he looked up, she couldn't tell if he was sincere, or simply making another play for her affection. "If you ever need a shoulder…"

Jackson returned minutes before supper, a deep scowl in place of a wink, but Barbara managed to avoid him the entire evening and for two days thereafter. Keeping her mind on more pleasant activities, the days passed in happy confusion with them seeing each other only briefly at meals and sometimes not even then. She'd received a note from her mother that Cincinnati had called again. Ideas swirled in her head. If she took that engagement, she would be away from Jackson. He didn't want her anyway, did he?

Oh, why was life as an adult so confusing? She must decide what she really wanted. Convincing Jackson that he loved her, or going home to a singing career. Her singing had been the reason she'd broken it off with Elliott. No. She broke up with Elliott because of Jackson and if he would admit to loving her, she'd marry him, and he wouldn't make her choose. Anyway, there were rumors that talks were taking place in Chattanooga about its own Opera house. Couldn't she love Jackson *and* sing?

Gifts arrived daily and the dining room had been converted to *present* headquarters. Gifts on the table, large and small packages on the sideboard, even presents on the plant table once the violets were removed. Betty squealed and clapped her hands as the wrappings fell away. "Just what I wanted."

Two days and counting. Final touches added to the perfect details. The fruit pies and honey cakes remained in the cold cellar until the last minute so they would be fresh when served. Pounds of peanut brittle waited in tins to keep them dry. Molly planned to arrive late Friday after-

noon to roast two plump turkeys, a dozen fat-as-butter
chickens and four fresh pork shoulders. Mrs. Schroeder
had offered to bring two ten-pound venison roasts, spiced
with her secret seasonings. Aunt Jenny drew the short
straw for three roaster pans of scalloped potatoes and two
of corn pudding. Barbara hoped Aunt Jenny would add
a touch of sugar and onion to the corn like Aunt Ina. At
least onion.

A real country wedding. With the war, the family didn't
think it proper to go all out, renting a hall and spending
money that could be put to better use for the soldiers, al-
though white wooden chairs had been rented from the
church, enough for two hundred people.

According to Betty, that meant half the town intended to
come. Some would sit. A few would just have to stand. Barbara liked the informality compared to what she was sure
the VanDusens would have planned for her. She thanked
God every day she hadn't walked down that aisle. Because
marriage was for life, for better or worse. Probably lots of
for worse, but why start out that way?

Teddy's parents were expected to arrive tomorrow, and
Barbara did her best to help put the house in order, not
that she'd ever seen it out of order. Confirmed reserva-
tions waited at the hotel for Mr. and Mrs. Barrymore. Teo
and Teddy already had rooms, though they'd stayed there
very little. Teddy couldn't be pried from Betty's side and
Teo had found himself content to dog Barbara's heels, to
her chagrin.

According to the *Farmer's Almanac,* unseasonably dry
weather for the rest of the month answered their prayers,
so the crepe paper streamers appeared that morning.
Thursday night, Barbara worked until she fell into bed
exhausted, but in a good way.

"Betty, can you believe it? Two more days and you'll

be Mrs. Theodore Barrymore. Say, that rhymes. I didn't notice until now." How strange it must feel to be a bride. "Are you all right?"

"I'm a little scared. With all the excitement about the wedding, I never gave much thought to being Mrs. Anybody. How odd that will be. I've been happy simply being Elizabeth Judge. Now to be Teddy's wife. I'm on clouds."

Barbara shifted so she faced Betty's twin bed. "You really love him, don't you?"

The stillness swallowed both of them until Betty broke the silence with soft, gentle, almost embarrassed words. "Of course I do. I couldn't even think of marrying someone if I didn't love him." Her face flashed crimson. "Did you love Elliott? Truly love him? I couldn't tell from your letters."

Biting down on her lip, recalling the short engagement, Barbara figured honesty between friends was good. "I thought I did. Until I came to New Hope with my family."

Betty flipped so her chin rested in her hands. "What changed your mind?"

"I met your brother."

Betty's eyes widened with mischief. "Will?"

"Of course not, silly."

Giggling, Betty punched the pillow.

"He winked at me through the car window when he came to help Father." The memory brought a smile to her lips.

"He winks at all the girls."

Barbara swiveled onto her back, hugged the pillow to her chest and stared at the ceiling. "I know that now. But then, I thought he was being fresh." She squeezed the pillow harder. "And sort of cute. Enough that I couldn't keep my eyes off him. Much as I hate to admit it, I've loved your brother for a year and a half. And he's not so much as scribbled a line on one of your letters or given me a word of encouragement in all that time."

Betty's voice lowered. "Remember what I told you? He gave you the hair combs he'd bought for Grand. He hasn't done anything so strange as long as I've known him. I think he likes you, too. Or did." She shook her head until curls danced across her brow and tickled the fingers supporting her face. "I'm not sure he likes himself right now."

Jackson stared at the shadows the light outside his window made across the ceiling. The cracks had resembled animals when he was small, now they hovered. Instead of a lion, a bear and a crow, they were demons screaming his name, branding him a coward, laughing at him. They had bodies like animals, but their faces resembled Teo Barrymore.

One day at a time. Smile and bow. Kneel and pray. Grin and shake hands. All the rituals expected of him for his sister's wedding.

Noise downstairs. Will must still be up. Their parents would be furious if his brother made a mess. He slipped on his Levi's and tugged a T-shirt over his head. Taking the stairs two at a time, he stole to the parlor.

"C'mon, Will. A little more won't hurt."

"I said I don't drink, Teo." Feet scuffled.

"You did after the movie."

"Not on purpose. Why don't you go to your hotel?"

Jack peered around the corner, not wanting to step on Will's toes. At seventeen, the boy was old enough to handle this himself.

Teo dropped the flask in his pocket and turned. "You and your holier-than-thou family need to lighten up a bit. I've never met anyone as uptight as you and your sister. And that brother of yours—"

"You called?" Jackson swallowed down the anger before stepping into view. Entering the room he said, "Like Will told you, I think it's time for you to leave, Teo."

"Hey, old man. Didn't hear you skulking around." He pulled out the flask. "How about letting bygones be bygones? Here, have a nip."

Jackson crept a step closer. "Out of the house." He glanced toward the stairs and lowered his voice. "There won't be any bygones."

Teo strode nearer Jackson's side. "I've never understood that, Jack, my boy. I haven't done a thing to you."

Blood pounded in Jackson's ears. He glanced over at Will whose face had gone white. This was his fight alone. One he didn't plan on losing. He inched forward, fists at his sides, and Teo immediately stepped back.

Jackson let the words slip out a threat. "I won't have you spoiling the wedding. And you know very well what you did to that girl."

"Don't have a clue, buddy-boy, but for Betty's sake and everyone else's, we should probably forget the past and move on. You don't want the wedding spoiled for that pretty little sister of yours, now do you?" He stuffed the flask back in his pocket.

Will's eyes narrowed. "Jack? Can I help?"

"Go on upstairs."

Jackson stood in place like a granite wall until Will was out of earshot. "Let's go, Teo." With fists tightening at his sides, he moved forward.

"You have interfered in my life one too many times, Jackson. Make this the last."

Teo's fist rose inches under Jackson's nose, but Jack was quicker. With the swiftest flick of his wrist, he wrenched Teo's hand, pressing the fingers down hard against Teo's arm.

"I said enough! I may look like a patsy, but, Teo, you're wrangling with the wrong man. Keep your distance from my sister, from her friend and from my family in general. Just do what you have to do for the wedding and get out of New Hope."

Teo didn't say a word, just stared at Jackson's face. Jerking free of his grasp, Teo turned and marched to the door. In less than a second, he was gone.

A few moments passed while Jackson leaned on the table, his head down. He was messing things up but royally. And Betty's wedding would feel the brunt of his anger. Noise came from behind him. He flew around, fists up and ready. Will.

His hands dropped as his kid brother drew closer. Jackson smiled, touched Will's shoulder. "You okay, kid?"

Will's head hung, shame an unwelcome companion for the Judge men. "I am now. I really didn't know he put alcohol in my soda at the movies. I thought it tasted kinda funny, but I've never had anything to drink before. Don't tell Dad."

"S'okay, kid. I know you." Clasping an arm around Will's shoulder, he mumbled, "You handled yourself all right. Like a man. I'm proud of you."

Red-faced, but grinning, Will said, "Thanks."

Chapter 12

Friday night ushered in another round of celebration. The Barrymores had arranged for a truckload of goodies to be shipped from Chattanooga for the rehearsal dinner. Everything from food to linens to stemware had been packaged and delivered to the church fellowship hall which would serve as the dining room.

Jackson wondered how they had worked around the rationing. Oh, well, they were a good lot, really. Except for their older son. But, of course, no one else knew the truth about him. And could never know for Ted and Betty's sakes.

Jackson helped unload the dinner boxes before heading back to the house for the actual rehearsal.

Wedding participants arrived at the Judges' home around five. Jackson leaned against the back porch and watched them all flapping about, doing their best to get the order right the first time through, but all he pictured was a gaggle of geese scurrying back and forth, feathers flying and beaks honking. He snorted back a chuckle.

His eyes never left sight of Teo: Teo walking Barbara down the aisle, Teo escorting her through the house, Teo offering to drive her to the church.

And the lady showed no signs of protesting.

"Thank you, Teo. You're such a gentleman."

Ha. Her behavior was enough to make him lose his lunch especially when she let her gaze slide from Teo to him.

What happened to her ability to put a man in his place? Well, he'd watch out for her safety whether she did or not.

Will swung alongside and leaned on Jackson's shoulder. "How long you gonna let that go on?" Teo and Barbara laughed at some stupid joke. "Probably outta stop it. You know what he's like."

"I do know." Jackson realized too clearly that his brother still stung from last night's humiliation.

He pulled Will's hand from his shoulder. "But you, little brother, had better get back. Be a voice of sanity for both of us, okay?" *And help me keep close watch over Barbara.*

Convinced Jackson had been spying when Teo escorted her out by the arm, Barbara glanced over her shoulder. No. He didn't appear to care at all. A bit of guilt about egging Teo on in order to make Jackson jealous stabbed her heart. The deceit rose in her throat and she swallowed it down, pretending she didn't have a clue where the shame came from. There was a name for girls like this, but she wasn't *really* leading Teo on. Was she? She only wanted Jackson to notice her. Admit he loved her. That wasn't teasing, was it?

Warning bells she chose to ignore clanged in her head. Just 'til after the wedding and then, if Jackson didn't get

the message, she'd let Teo know she had no interest in him.
A sort of game. Men played games all the time.

Betty dashed beside her. "Come on, you two. You're
going in the lead car. The place of honor."

Teo hesitated, looked around, frowned. "But I
thought—"

Teddy punched Teo in the arm. "Then you thought
wrong, big brother. You and Barbara are guests of honor.
Next to us, of course. Let's go." He hauled Teo across the
yard, out of Barbara's reach.

In a matter of minutes, all four tumbled from the car
and entered the church, Betty and Barbara singing their
favorite songs at the top of their voices, arms linked like
the best friends they were.

Wonderful scents filtered through the air. "C'mon,"
Barbara called, hungry as usual. "Let's find dinner."

"Barbara, how do you stay so slim?" Betty gazed in
her direction. "I'd be as big as Auntie if I ate like you."

Teo leaned in. "Seems to work well for you."

She rolled her eyes.

Two gentlemen in white jackets waited to serve the
guests. Pastor McConnaughey offered the prayer and soon
everyone dug into chilled lobster salad and crusty rolls.
Barbara savored each bite. She hadn't tasted anything
so delicious before. This must have cost the Barrymores
more than the church budget for a month. Of course, she
wouldn't ask, but she enjoyed seeing how the other half
lived. How she might have lived.

She looked up and squirmed in her seat. Jackson hadn't
taken his eyes from her all night. He glanced her direction
when Teo repeated a joke, hoping for a second round of
laughs. He stared when Teo leaned toward her to answer a
question. And he glared when Teo dared touch her arm in

response to a story she had told him. The plan was working better than she'd expected.

If only he'd look away for a minute. Stop his intense scrutiny of her every move. Well, wasn't that what she had wanted? Her emotions swam through her head in dizzying circles.

And he didn't stare like he wanted to tear Teo apart; he had the audacity to smirk at them. Well, she'd put a stop to this silly game. She'd made her point. He did care about her. And once the wedding was over, she'd be done with Teo.

After delicate fruit tarts, tea and coffee had been served, Barbara excused herself and stepped onto the porch of the church, hoping Jackson would follow suit.

The deep voice. His presence unmistakable as he drew up behind her. "Are you really such a little fool?" His fingers, like talons on her arm, speared the tender skin.

She attempted to slip away, but his grip tightened and spun her to him. She knew better than to fight against his angry grasp. Trapped in his hold, she waited.

He glared, but no words accompanied the expression. Looking away so she didn't have to feel the rage emanating from his eyes, she held back. She couldn't very well deny she'd played the part of a fool.

Finally, he leaned toward her ever so slightly. She was sure he was going to kiss her. Maybe he'd admit he loved her. All the worries she'd harbored would be gone. She closed her eyes, held her breath and hoped.

Instead, he whispered close enough to her ear that she felt the warmth of his breath on her cheek and neck. "In games, Barbara, there are winners and losers. Nothing in between. I'll say this only once." Warmth or no warmth, she shivered. "Don't be the loser in Teo's game." He lifted her to her toes. Her eyes popped open so she had to stare him in the face. "You have no idea how well Teo plays."

Betty giggled until tears poured from her eyes. At this rate, they weren't likely to get any sleep. Barbara had escaped being alone with Teo because they'd ridden home with Betty and Ted. She hadn't seen Jackson again after his warning.

Too much excitement for one night. But her main job as maid of honor was to keep Betty happy. All thoughts of Teo and Jackson disappeared once Betty started talking. "A new car. A 1942 Ford Super dee-luxe convertible. Wasn't she beautiful?"

Barbara could barely believe the Barrymores' gift. But then again, the Judges had given the couple a whole *house*. Barbara had breathed a sigh of relief seeing their smiles when she had given the couple the Breitling watches, convinced they loved them as much as the car.

Betty exhaled with a dreamy sigh and gave the faraway look Barbara recognized as thoughts of Teddy. "Barbara, could I ask a huge favor? I don't think I'm ever going to sleep. If you happen to be going downstairs, maybe get me some warm milk?"

"Ooh. She thinks she's the Queen of England. Your wish is my command." And with a deep bow, Barbara shot her a look. They started giggling all over again as Barbara slipped into her slacks and a sweater.

She pulled the sweater close against the unexpected chill and drew on fuzzy mules from under her bed. "Give me a minute. And if you're asleep when I get back…well, I'll think of something *dire* to do to you."

"Not dire. Not the night before my wedding." Betty threw her pillow and fell off the side of the bed. "Oh, look at the mess I'm making." She clamored back under the quilts and pulled them up to her chin, a childish grin deepening her dimples. "I guess after tonight, I have to grow up whether I want to or not."

Barbara crept to the kitchen and checked around the edges of the door. No light on. Glad she wouldn't have to face Jackson, she slipped inside as quietly as possible. It took a few seconds for her eyes to adjust.

And her nose to catch a whiff of fresh coffee and... Jackson. Holding a cup and a cookie, he sat in the dark.

"I didn't see a light. Sorry. Betty asked for some warm milk."

He didn't utter a word. Just sipped his coffee.

She opened the refrigerator and poured milk into the pan. This was becoming a nightly ritual. "I'll leave in a minute."

He lifted the cup to his lips. "Fine with me."

"It was a lovely dinner, wasn't it?"

"As dinners go." Jackson wiped his mouth, rose and strolled to the window overlooking the gazebo.

"You're teasing, right? I mean, lobster and those fruit tarts. I've never in my life tasted anything so delicious."

Finally turning her back on him, Barbara stirred the milk so it wouldn't scorch. "I think it's going to be a beautiful wedding." She chewed the edge of her lip. This silent treatment drove her crazy and was so unfair. "I'm happy for them. Aren't you?"

Nothing.

Fire rose in her belly. He couldn't be more rude if he had hung out a sign that said *Barbara Richardson, go home.* "But then again, *they* understand the concept of love, don't they? Of course *they* will be happy. Why not? It's not as if *they* pretend the other doesn't exist." She put down the spoon and stomped her foot, eyes glaring into his back. Anger, anything would be better than ignoring her this way. "Well, what do you have to say for yourself?"

He turned, stared long and hard at her. Electricity sparked in the air until Barbara swore the earth trembled.

The clock in the parlor struck midnight, jarring the silence. His lip curled, brows slanted down, deep—deeper. In two strides, he covered the distance between them. With one motion, he grasped her arm and pulled her close. Thunder poured from his mouth. "Listen to me. Find someone who can give you everything you deserve. A good life. That person isn't me. I don't love you." His fingers tightened. "Please, leave me alone."

Her fingers quickly sought to cover his hand. "I know why you're doing this. Jackson, no one who loves you cares about a couple of scars."

He pushed her from him. "A couple of scars?" Whipping up his shirt sleeves and holding his arms in front of her face, he said, "Look at me. My hands. My arms." He ran fingers over the scar on his forehead. "My face."

"No one thinks you're different, Jackson. No one but yourself."

His laugh came out a hideous rumble and frightened her. He seemed to change before her eyes. *Oh, Jackson. Why can't you get past this pain?*

Her heart slammed into her ribs and beat with an abnormal rhythm. Breaths exploded in her lungs and she fought to control and steady them. She had to think. Say the right thing or scare him off for good.

"Jackson." She reached out with shaking fingers and traced the scar that ran the length of his face. When she came to his lip, she fluttered her fingers over the cut. "I'm sorry this haunts you, but it's only a wound. One that will heal given enough time. I'm a firm believer all things happen for a reason."

"Barbara, stop." He reached for her hand and tried to pull it away.

But she wouldn't budge. He had to know she wasn't afraid to touch him. She kissed her fingertips and skimmed them across the scar on his mouth. Then she leaned in.

Make her stop, Lord. I can only take so much. He spun away from the gentle touch. Walked back to the window. Accepted his fate. A life alone, without Barbara. "They happen for a reason all right. So men of power could take what they wanted."

The burner sputtered and died before he heard her step toward the window—and him. Long arms wrapped from his back to his chest. He felt her face press into the fabric of his shirt. She stayed, her cheek to his back, until her warmth eased through the cotton shirt and calmed him. If only he could allow her to remain right there for the rest of her life. Those were selfish dreams. Maybe she would change her mind when she returned home. After all, Elliott VanDusen could give her so much. They might run away to New York so his business would grow and she could sing on stage.

No, that wasn't Barbara. She might want to sing, but she wasn't some prima donna who needed money and prestige.

"You tried to help, Jackson." Her words hummed against his back. "All any of us can do is try. You're so hard on yourself."

His muscles stiffened under her chin. She'd said enough. But he couldn't walk away. He loved this woman more than his own flesh and wished he could let her help him get through life. But he loved her too much to let her wither away with him.

When she tightened her grip from behind him, her palms pressed into his chest. If she tightened them any more, he'd surrender. Jackson drew in a deep breath and held it. The sudden rush of air over his lips vaulted him to action. His hands eased over hers and lifted the soft fingers from his chest. He put palms against the window frame and leaned away from her. This was his last chance to dissuade her.

Keeping his back to her, he said, "You should take Betty her warm milk."

Chapter 13

Saturday morning broke sunny and clear. Not a cloud in the sky. Today was the day. Jackson would have to put on his best smile. No one else had to be in on the secret—his actions were all pretense.

He walked to the closet. Opened the doors. Took out his suit. He eyed the top shelf and gently lifted down the glove. Small. Her hands had been tiny next to his. He'd thought himself in love for the first time. And when she had agreed to go to the graduation dance with him, he had soared.

In her blue dress with little white gloves, she'd looked like a princess. And he'd felt like the king of the dance. Now, he wondered, had she agreed to go so she could get closer to Ted's brother, Teo? One question that wasn't answered; he never saw her again after she left the dance with Teo that night.

"Jackson, wake up. Time to get a move on." His father's steps sounded lively as he moved along the hall, rapping on doors, announcing the obvious. "Big day, big day. Up 'n' at 'em."

Jackson tossed the glove back on the shelf, putting an end to bad memories. He pulled his suit from the closet and brushed at an imaginary piece of lint. Anything to keep his mind on the day and not his ghosts.

Donning work pants and a flannel shirt for last-minute chores, he sat on the bed. He opened the nightstand drawer, pushed the packs of gum aside and pulled out his dog tags. The hard ridges of his name and number tingled the raw nerves in his fingers. Jackson Lee Judge. Good Southern name. Good fighting man's name. He'd fought the good fight, isn't that what Barbara had said? As opposed to what? A bad fight? The tags slipped to the floor.

Ollie's tags had been in his hand. And they'd slipped through, too. Only Ollie had depended on Jackson to hang on. Hold him. Save him. Pull him from the burning water. With a kid's faith, he had held his breath and plunged under the fiery wreckage until Jackson could support him under the arms and lift, but all Jackson hung onto was a scrap of shirt and tags.

After a few seconds of quiet, he lifted his boot and slammed it on top of his own IDs.

Betty had fallen asleep by the time Barbara had returned to the bedroom the night before. A gentle snore had emanated from the bride-to-be's side of the room and Barbara had laughed in spite of the sadness that had lingered from her conversation with Jackson. Laughing had felt good after such a serious discussion. And she had laughed, only her heart wasn't in it.

Only God could change a heart. When had Jackson officially stepped away from God? Perhaps it had been a gradual process. War did strange things to people.

She would smile and laugh for Betty's sake today. Any day other than today and Bets would have noticed the difference, but this day her friend would have tunnel vision.

Glancing at the sleeping bride-to-be, Barbara decided she had a job to concentrate on. Roll Betty out of bed and play the part of drill sergeant. "Up and at 'em. Let's go. Time to wake up." She jiggled the bed, finally grabbing the edge of the sheet and yanking. "Time for breakfast. A bubble bath. We'll fix your hair and slide you into the beautiful gown hanging in the guest room closet. Let's go see if we can help your mother flip a few pancakes. Anything to get you married and get me—"

"Get you what?"

"In trouble if I don't have you out of bed, dressed and down the stairs in time for breakfast."

The rest of the morning flew by in preparations. Betty's gown fit perfectly and Barbara adjusted the veil for the fifth time, admiring Betty in her cheval mirror. Her hair in soft loose curls looked so lovely Barbara hated to cover it. Mrs. Judge teared up and had to step away for a second.

Betty touched a hand to her mother's arm. "We should join the others, Mother."

"I know. I've waited for this day and now it's here, I'm not sure how I'll ever get through it." She dabbed her eyes as she handed Betty the beautiful bouquet of blossoms. "Betty, you are the most beautiful bride."

Barbara noticed Mrs. Judge had even lost her habit of ending every sentence with a question. At the bottom of the stairs, all the men but Teddy waited patiently. They had only a short distance to walk through to the back, but everyone had to be in their planned positions and start together. Once they arrived at the back of the house, Barbara took Teo's arm, and she didn't miss Jackson's tight jaw when Teo leaned in and told her how gorgeous she looked. Maybe if Jackson would pay her a tad of attention, she could free herself of the pompous Frenchman.

At last, it was Betty's turn, accompanied by Mr. Judge. Little Ellen Sue Schroeder in her miniature version of the bride's gown tossed flower petals, stopped, picked them up and then threw them again, taking her a good five minutes to go the full length of the path.

Mr. Judge leaned in and kissed Betty on the forehead. He was so much like her own father. Barbara fought back tears thinking of her family.

Once Betty and her father arrived in the front, Teddy dwarfed her hand in his as they both stood, side by side, under the garden gazebo, thick and white with blossoms. The flowers filled the air with the sweetest odors. Lily of the valley had been tucked into bunches in the tulle and the first blushes of white lilacs peeked around the bows on either side of them.

The minister spoke so softly at first, Barbara strained to hear the words.

"…in sickness and in health."

In sickness. I'd take care of you, Jackson, no matter what happened. I love you. Want to be part of your life. Can't you see that?

"…to love and to cherish."

I'd cherish you, Jackson. All the days of my life. Right by your side no matter what.

Jackson cleared his throat. Discomfort seeped from his pores and he wiped his forehead. The sooner this ended, the better. He glanced over at Teo, eyes glued to the bodice of Barbara's dress. Jackson gritted his teeth, tighter and tighter. For now, his jaw muscles twitched until they hurt. If only he and Barbara…

"…in sickness and in health."

Be realistic. Will my back get stronger with time or give out from the injury? If it gets worse, will I be able to hold a job, support a family? "…to love and to cherish."

I love you, Barbara, and I've cherished you from that first glance through the car window. I'll always love you, but you deserve better than a broken man like me.

"…until death do you part."

Until death.

If Teo grabbed her arm one more time, Barbara would slap him across his smug face. She drew in a deep breath and tried not to think about the loathsome man standing beside her at the punch bowl. All through the service, each time she had looked up, he had leered at her. He was apparently still under the misconception that she had an interest in him. That had to stop.

Soon, the guests would all leave. She could make clear to Teo how she felt. For now, it was time to relax—something she hadn't been able to do since they were matched as wedding partners. But for the rest of the evening she had to at least be agreeable.

"Certainly was a lovely wedding," she said. The blossom-covered gazebo took her breath away.

Teo held his hand against her elbow. "You were lovely. I couldn't care less about weddings."

All night Jackson had watched her every move. Almost as if he had guarded her from afar. Why? Teo was a boor, but harmless. She'd dealt with worse in New Castle where her affluent high school had been filled with one smug character after another. After enrolling and attending for a month, she had wished she could have stayed with her friends at the old school. The private school, as she had learned, was filled with privilege. Not exactly her style.

She covered her lips as a laugh slipped from her mouth.

She remembered the braggart, Glenn Bassett, she had bowled with one Friday night in July. In his white duck pants, he'd pranced around the alley, flexing his muscles, smiling for all the girls. He was a popular fellow. When at last it had come time for Glenn to bowl, he'd edged to the line, looked over his shoulder and winked at her. Then, with a large wind up, he threw the ball. Only his feet didn't cooperate as they should have and he lost his footing, slipping all the way down the alley in those white pants. She'd laughed until she had cried. Nice guy, but what a show-off. A good sport, though. When he had stood, he raised both hands in the air and pranced around the pins as if he'd just trounced Joe Louis.

A voice on her other side caught her attention. Jackson. "You were smiling. Something funny you'd like to share?"

"Not really." As soon as the words left her mouth, she realized he'd been trying to be sociable. He looked hurt.

Here she stood in front of a table laden with food, Jackson scowling on one side, the pompous Frenchman on the other. Trapped like a rabbit with no hole to hide in.

While it was obvious no love was lost between the two men, Jackson carried his dislike to a whole other level. She moved, he moved. She went for punch, he went for punch. All the while, Teo followed as the third to be sure Barbara didn't leave with Jackson. Smothered by them long enough, Barbara grabbed her shawl and slipped into the house, powdering her nose as a ruse.

Later, past the guests at the gazebo, she stumbled upon Jackson's brother. "Hey, Barbara. What are you up to?"

"Oh, just going for a walk, Will."

"Alone in the dark?"

She leaned forward, plastered on a wide grin and said, "*All* alone." She pecked his cheek, getting the desired reaction. A red blush zapped his cheeks. "Don't worry, Will. Just need to clear the cobwebs."

She sailed past the men smoking cigars farther along the path, and beyond the treelike bushes of lilacs blooming profusely after the hot day. A quick peek over her shoulder showed a clean getaway. She should be ashamed; Jackson would be worrying and angry. Teo, insulted and incensed. Too bad. Those men suffocated her.

Listening to the night sounds, she felt her tension drain from the muscles in her neck all the way down her shoulders, into her arms, and finally her hands. Fingers flexing, she realized how stressed the men had made her. The clear, starry night belonged to her now.

Pink and delicate, wild roses grew in thick bushes along the path. She stooped to pick a handful, breathing in the heady scent. One of the leaves tickled her nose.

She continued along the worn path until before she knew it, she'd walked across the Judges' property from the front to the back. Still, she could think of nothing but Jackson.

Oh, she'd messed everything up with her attempt to make him jealous. All it had done was bring out his anger and rightfully so. She should have listened when that small voice told her not to be deceitful.

Wanting to hide from God like Adam in the garden, she sauntered around the peach tree and slumped to the ground, a blanket of soft grass for a seat. It hadn't worked for Adam; the plan had backfired on her.

Twigs snapped. She stopped and listened. Footsteps, heavy and close. Jackson, no doubt acting as her protector. At least that part of their relationship seemed to be inevitable.

The sound of a knee cracking, someone kneeling behind her. A soft whisper. "What are you thinking?"

Maybe he'd come to his senses. She plastered on a huge smile and turned. "That you don't need to follow me around like—Teo?"

Looking into Teo's face, unable to hide her disappointment, she figured now was as good a time as any to come clean.

"Who were you expecting?" He stood to his feet, towering over her like a dark shadow. Though his smile remained in place, something wasn't right.

Stomach churning, instincts on alert, she rose.

"Is something the matter?" He offered his hand. "I thought we were having a good time."

"No. I..." The churning switched to a steady burn that threatened to rise in her throat. He shouldn't be here; she shouldn't, either. Darkness had wholly settled in and she was so far from the backyard, she couldn't see the lights behind the house anymore. "Just too many people. I thought I'd take a walk. Maybe we should return." She smiled, moved to duck under the limb, but smaller branches clustered, preventing escape.

Teo pressed forward until an arm reached around each side of her, the tree trapping her and making flight impossible as he leaned in. "I rather like the solitude, don't you?"

"I think maybe we should go back, Teo. I picked these flowers. Would you help me carry them?" She bent to retrieve the spray, but he grabbed her arm.

His solid body didn't budge. Her heart pounded so loud, he must be able to hear and know she was afraid. "Teo. Let's get back." Her face tightened as she looked around for a place to run. "Please."

"That's not what you've been saying all week." His hand circled her neck.

Why had she left the party? Her hands trembled as she grasped his arms, dug in and pushed as hard as she could. His grip didn't lessen one bit. In fact, he tightened his hold on her.

"I want you to leave me alone."

"I want. I want. You're so self-centered, Barbara. Always thinking of yourself. How about what I want?"

"Please. I'm sorry if I led you on."

"You weren't just leading me on. I know true feelings when I see them."

"You're wrong."

He was stronger, bigger and she had walked too far from the house. They must be more than a half mile away. What could she do? He might not be able to hold on if she slipped to the ground—dead weight; then maybe she would have a chance to get up and run. She drew in a deep breath and dropped against his grasp. Free for only a second. Teo was there when she jumped up, hands snatching for her shoulders once again. He played with her like a cat might a helpless, frightened mouse.

"Please, go away!"

Teo's face contorted. "Now listen here."

A moment's silence lay thick between them as if time had suspended.

Deep, heavy breathing like someone who'd been running. "No. You listen."

The voice. Barbara whipped around—Jackson. Now her heart tripped in her chest, but without the fear. He moved closer, his face a mixture of anger and pain. "Leave…the lady…alone."

Teo's eyes narrowed. He stepped away from Barbara. "You use the word *lady* lightly, old man. You've seen her fawning over me all week. Led me out here so we could be alone. Or maybe you think she's interested in you?"

Barbara ducked just in time. Jackson's fist sailed through the air and drove into the middle of Teo's face.

Like a wounded bear with its foot in a trap, he bellowed, but Jackson proved relentless. Barbara stayed out of the way by hiding on the other side of the tree. Yet, she couldn't stop watching.

Jackson grabbed the front of Teo's jacket and with one hand lifted the Frenchman off his feet. "Apologize to the *lady!*"

Though his face was cut and bleeding, Teo managed to slur out the words, "Not on your life. I'm not apologizing to—"

Whack. Jackson released his grip as Teo fell to his knees.

"S-sorry, Barbara."

She covered her mouth with her hand to keep from crying out. *Please, God. Don't let Jackson get hurt. This is all my fault.*

Jackson wedged himself between Teo and Barbara. "I think you should leave."

Teo rose, his eyes locked on to Jackson's and he limped away, clutching his stomach. Once out of Jackson's reach, Teo yelled, "We'll finish this, Jack. This has been a long time coming and it's not over between us."

Jackson stood, feet shoulder width apart, his muscles tensed and ready. "You can't run away, Teo. And you'll never hurt another woman as long as you live. So help me."

Teo shouted over his shoulder, "You help yourself, you pathetic freak. Don't worry about me. I've always been able to get whatever girl I want. Remember?"

Jackson went rigid, his arms like bars of steel. Barbara wasn't sure what Teo had meant. Whatever, Jackson was angrier than she'd ever seen a man.

To keep him from following Teo, she wrapped her arms around Jackson's neck. He looked from Teo's fading figure back into her eyes and crushed her to him. His words like rain on fire to her ears. "You all right?"

Burying her face in his chest, she said, "Now, I am."

"If anything happened to you I don't know what I'd do."

"Don't worry. I'm fine."

As soon as she said she was fine, she looked up. His face darkened. He slipped her hands from around his neck, his forehead creased in a scowl deeper than the Mississippi. He spoke low like he might speak to a child who'd been caught misbehaving. "Barbara, listen to me and listen good. As a woman, you have every right to say no to a man, but with rights come responsibilities. You've been telling Teo *yes* all week long. Men are simple creatures. We believe what we think we hear and Teo thought you were telling him that you were very interested in him."

She tried to contradict him but words, honest words, wouldn't come. She tried again to hold him, feel safe in his arms.

"What did you expect him to think?"

"What? How can you say that? This is my fault?"

"No. He should have respected you when you told him to leave. But you can't play with people's emotions. If I hadn't come along when I did—"

Jackson removed his jacket and placed it around her shoulders. Then he turned and stalked away, Barbara stumbling along behind him.

"Jack, wait."

"I think it's way past time."

"Time for what?"

"For you to grow up, Barbara."

Women. If he lived to be a thousand… What did she think Teo would do? Hug her? Hold her? Protect her? Show her respect? She couldn't have been more wrong. Jackson stormed into the backyard, watching all the time for Barbara to catch up. If Will hadn't told him where she'd gone, this story might have had a much different ending.

Ted was a terrific guy. How had the Barrymores whelped such a louse as Teo? Maybe he'd been the favorite and spoiled. Jackson had seen worse at school. Privileged boys from good homes, with parents who'd told them all their lives how wonderful they were. Planted the belief in their heads that they were entitled—to whatever they wanted.

Barbara slunk around the corner of the gazebo with tears in her eyes. Jackson wanted nothing more than to take her in his arms and convince her it would be all right. All was forgiven. But it wasn't. The game she'd been playing this week had been dangerous for each of them.

Barbara dashed past the few remaining guests to her room before anyone else could stop her—question her. Tears burned hot on her cheeks. Jackson had only told the truth. She'd been playing with fire all week to make Jackson jealous, and her immature behavior had blown up in her face. Her mother had warned her about such conduct and God had warned her with His written words. *Not by deceit.* Now, it was too late.

She fingered the soft wool of Jackson's suit coat, drew it closer around her, trembling under the blanket of warmth. She turned her nose into the fabric and breathed in the fragrance. Ivory soap and the light, lingering aroma of the peach blossoms swirled together and filled her senses along with the unmistakable scent of Jackson himself. With her arms wrapped across her chest, she pretended Jackson held her. But it wasn't his arms. Just an old coat that she took off.

She shivered. Teo had threatened Jackson. He might make good that threat.

None of it mattered. In two days she would be gone. Back to New Castle, Indiana, where her family waited. She could forget about all men and concentrate on her singing.

Chapter 14

Over the delicious aroma of crisp bacon and warm maple syrup, Mr. Judge's brow arched up as he stared across the table at Jackson. "I heard there was a bit of a tussle last night." His head dipped to his plate of food.

Barbara glanced from Jackson to his father. No one could miss the black and blue tinge across the back of Jackson's knuckles when he lifted a cup to his lips. The entire family must have heard by now what a fool she'd made of herself.

Jackson set the cup down, slumped on his elbow and pressed against the table, but his face reflected directness as he sought his father's eyes. "No, sir, just a slight misunderstanding."

"One that might cause problems for Teddy and Bets?"

"Dad, Teo and I will never be friends, but I won't allow that to affect my sister's happiness. If we have to be in each other's company for whatever reason, I'll behave if Teo does. However, if he takes advantage of situations, then I'll step in to right the wrong. The choice is pretty much his."

Mr. Judge clapped his hands together. "Well, then, let's have our breakfast and put any unpleasantries behind us."

Barbara cringed; she'd been the root of the *unpleasantries*. She couldn't wait for the meal to finish so she could escape to her room and pack her belongings. Tomorrow she'd be on the train for home. *Home.*

She missed Betty already. The two lovebirds had taken the first train out this morning, practically before the sun rose. And there was no longer a reason for her to stay.

Was that a smile edging her face? Why not, impatience probably ran from her head to her toes. She couldn't wait to leave this house. Get away from him. She had no doubt been counting the days since she had arrived and had seen him.

"Jackson, are you with us? Could you please pass the syrup to Barbara?" Mother's face quizzed him. "French toast is a bit dry without it, don't you think?"

Startled, Jackson picked up the blue willow pitcher and reached toward Barbara's outstretched hand. His fingers brushed hers in the transfer and he choked on the coffee swirling in his mouth. He shifted back in his seat and mopped at his shirt with a napkin.

His mother fired him a look.

"Sorry, Mother. I seem to be making one mess after another."

In twenty-four hours Barbara would be gone. Just one more day, but he couldn't figure out if that was what he really wanted or not. One thing was sure, he couldn't sit here in her presence and think straight.

Not hungry anymore, he pushed back his chair and stood up. "If you'll all excuse me, I'm heading out back to finish some of the cleaning. "Dad, when you're done eating, I'll help you pack up the chairs and we can return them to church. No rush, but I'll get started stacking."

Though he didn't intend to, he slammed the door leading out back. Surveying the mess gave him something else to concentrate on and he dug in.

Fifty, fifty-one, fifty-two. Jackson counted out piles of ten chairs each as he folded and stacked. Hard work kept his mind from Barbara. Sixty-six, sixty-seven. Sweat dripped in his eyes and he brushed at it using damp shirt sleeves as he started another pile. Fold and lift. Fold and lift. Seventy-two, seventy-three. He'd help his father and then he could take care of his own matters for a change. He had a life after all. Eighty-nine, ninety. No more worry about Miss Richardson. No more caring about who she chose to flirt with. Or who chose to flirt with her.

He stopped a minute, remembering her exchange with Teo. One hundred five, one hundred six. She could flirt with Errol Flynn if it pleased her. He couldn't care less.

Jackson leaned against the gazebo, catching his breath. Struggling, sweating, beating himself up on the outside. Nothing was going to take away what he felt inside. One hundred ten, one hundred eleven.

Just like before. He was seventeen again remembering how he and Teddy had unfolded dozens of chairs. Some were set up for the band, nearly one hundred for the other students, and a handful for the honored guests—teachers and parents serving as chaperones.

The parents shouldn't have been sitting in chairs. They should have been up, doing their jobs. Watching over the girls. Protecting them from jerks like Teo Barrymore.

Saturday night, the day before graduation, Jackson and Teddy had strolled proudly into the gym, two of the prettiest girls from school on their arms. Katherine O'Keefe had turned heads with her long red hair and laughing eyes. She'd removed her glove, dropped it in his pocket while they had danced. He wasn't sure, but by the end of the evening, he'd convinced himself he was falling in love.

He'd only turned his back for a couple minutes, just long enough to request her favorite song from the band. When he had returned to the dance floor, Teo swirled Katherine in his arms, covering the dance floor from one side to the other.

Jackson bent from his waist, lifted, groaned. Hefted another four chairs. He wiped more sweat away, doing his best to clear out memories that whorled through his mind like uninvited guests. A heave and up went another two chairs. He stopped, bit the edge of his lip, but pain couldn't wipe out memories so vivid he might reach out and touch them.

He'd dropped the cup of punch, strode across the floor. His jacket had been soaked through; he had taken it off and placed it on a chair near the door. The smells in the hot room had overwhelmed him for a minute. Cologne, sweat, stale food. He had grabbed the edge of the door frame and steadied himself. Looking out, he had to wonder where they'd gone.

She didn't return to school the next year. A girl's reputation was so easily shattered. Just the slightest hint of impropriety and a girl had faced ruin. A boy? His reputation had jumped up a notch or two. No. It wasn't fair. Jackson could see the inequity in that kind of reasoning.

One hundred ninety-nine.

Now, all that remained of her in New Hope was the small white glove he'd kept all these years in his coat pocket.

Last one. Two hundred. His lungs pushed out a rush of air. Done.

Barbara must have been as frightened as Katherine, and what did he do? Told her how foolish she'd been. Instead of holding her, as she'd wanted, he had chastised her for leading Teo on.

He shouldn't have talked to her the way he had in the peach grove. She'd known better than to egg Teo on. She didn't need Jackson rubbing her face in her folly.

There would be no train ride home today.

Clouds roiled as lightning struck again and again. Rain pounded the dry ground, which didn't seem to be able to soak it up fast enough. They were stuck inside until the rain stopped.

First thing that morning, her father's phone call to Mr. Judge confirmed what they'd heard on the radio. Dangerous high winds and driving rain had crisscrossed through Indiana, bringing with it deadly tornadoes. Could be zig-zagging into Ohio and Tennessee right now. Barbara's father had asked the Judges if Barbara might stay another week or so, until the weather stabilized and they could arrange to have their roof fixed. And while the Judges had agreed, Barbara ached to get home. She should be there, helping. Not here avoiding Jackson.

If Barbara had been wise, she'd have left for New Castle at the same time Betty and Ted left for their honeymoon. Instead, she'd offered early on to stay and help Mrs. Judge clean, press and put away the wedding clothes.

Now, hearing the news that she would have an extended visit, her legs, heavy and numb, carried her to her room as fast as she could make them go. With frustration as strong as the rain, she flopped on the bed and sobbed. Today was supposed to have been the day she finally escaped.

Grateful no one would hear her sobs over the lightning and thunder, she allowed herself the luxury of self-pity. Memories of another time, when flooding had caused them to stay, whirled in her head. *Brown eyes through a window. A new best friend. The kindness of strangers.* All memories that drew her back to New Hope. A sudden memory of her clothes flying through the air brought a much-needed smile to her lips. The event was funny now, but it certainly hadn't been then as she had scrambled to retrieve what Auntie Ina would call her unmentionables.

A crack of lightning pulled her attention to the window. She got up, wiped the last of the tears from her cheeks and stared into the black morning where only tiny glimpses of light fought to press through the weakest points in the clouds. In the anger of the storm, Barbara pictured a furrowed brow with eyes dark and foreboding, she put a hand to her throat, unsure where the storm outside started and the storm inside ended. She'd seen that face on Jackson the night he had confronted Teo on her behalf, when she had followed him to the lake. And she had witnessed the look when Jackson had chastised her for playing dangerous games.

Potato soup and corn bread with honey, his favorite, but even the tastiest meal couldn't straighten out the mess Jackson had made of his life. He couldn't change what happened at Pearl and now he had to deal with Barbara for another week.

That sure put a tack in his tire.

His mother passed the bowl again. "Another piece of corn bread?"

"Yeah."

"Are you all right, son? You've been moping around the house ever since Betty's wedding." She reached toward his hand, but he pulled away. A frown crossed her face. "Are you feeling well?"

"I'm fine." *Liar. Lying to yourself and now to your mother. This has to end.* "Really. I'll be fine."

His father looked at Mother and shook his head. "Leave the boy alone. He's not your baby anymore."

She shifted in her seat. "He'll always be my baby, like it or not. You know we're both here for you, don't you, Jackson?"

Jackson forced a smile. "I know."

"Say, Will's at the factory," his father said, "but where's Barbara? Not hungry? Not like her to miss a meal."

He groaned at the mention of her name.

His father looked up from his bowl. "You say something, son?"

"N-no. I, uh. No." He shoveled in more soup.

Once he'd excused himself, he dashed through the rain to the shed. Alone without all the questions. Tramping outside the building, he hauled in a few downed branches.

Then he appreciated the seclusion and dimness of the shed for the rest of the afternoon, slamming the ax into branches, one after another, letting his muscles labor until they burned. He hadn't carried such a heavy workload in a long while.

Rain pelted the roof, and lightning cracked against the old chestnut at the back of the house. They'd probably lose a few more branches before this storm passed. He stacked the wood in neat piles by the door. Will could take them out to season in the sun once the rain stopped.

For hours, slab after slab collapsed under the sharp sting of the ax. He couldn't believe his bad luck. Her staying longer changed his plans. Jackson slumped onto the growing pile of maple and chestnut; logs shifted and he lost his footing—landed in sawdust. Should he simply give up? Give in? Tell Barbara she meant more than the world to him?

Too many questions without answers. Leaning his head

against the wall, he daydreamed of porcelain skin, dark brown hair, and big—really big—blue eyes surrounded by thick, black lashes. A soft little mouth, almost always with an opinion to accompany the cuteness. He had to chuckle. She certainly *was* opinionated.

Sawdust sifted through his fingers and he snagged the edge of his lip between his teeth. He bit down hard because the pain felt good. It meant he was alive. He'd survived this horrible year, but he didn't want to dwell on his own survival. The thought of him living caused guilt to rise up in swells of disgrace. He should have died along with his friends.

If you truly loved someone, you let go. Allowed her to have a good life for herself. And he loved her enough to lift her up and let her wings take her away. He could see her on a stage, singing in that angelic voice. Pretending he didn't care took all his effort.

Why, God? Why can't she just go home where she belongs? I'm trying to do what's right here. Don't You ever listen to me?

No. No praying. He snatched a piece of wood and flung it as hard as he could against the shed wall. Boards shook and snatches of light peeked between them now that the rain had let up. God didn't care anyway.

The door opened and his father dipped his head under the five-foot door frame, a streak of sunlight doing its best to poke through the clouds. "Whoa, son. What are you doing? We don't want to have to repair the shed wall in all this muck and water. Your mother said to tell you, supper in about half an hour."

"Supper? We just had lunch."

"Five and a half hours ago. You've been here all afternoon. Maybe you should come in for a bit, get washed up, relax. The storm's had everyone on edge."

His father leaned down and offered a hand. "You don't seem happy, son." He tugged as Jackson heaved up on his heels. Then, he stared into Jackson's eyes. Was Father reading all the hurt?

"I'm happy enough just being with the family," he lied.

His father was no dummy. "If I didn't know any better, I'd say you weren't even glad you came back alive. Am I right?"

"Dad, I don't want to talk—"

"You know I'm here to listen when you do want to." He smiled and clapped Jackson on the back.

Once his father stepped away, Jackson brushed dirt from his palms and the seat of his pants. "Dad, I didn't want to talk about this before and I don't want to now." Wiping damp sawdust from the ax, he returned to the waiting pile of wood.

His father's brow lifted. "Festers, son."

"What?" Jackson set a log to split.

"Hurts fester inside if you don't talk it out."

Once his father left the shed, Jack put down the ax. The biceps in his right upper arm quivered, then spasmed from all the difficult work. He massaged the pain away and dropped to the floor again.

I don't want it to fester anymore, God. If You're there, really there so that You care about what happens to us, I need to know. Because if not, I'm finished fighting. Life is just too hard when it hurts this much. I'm destroying the people around me little by little. They'll be better off without me. So, I'm asking this last time. If I'm supposed to stay here for whatever reason, help me to understand it and see what I'm to do. If not, then let me go ahead with my plans.

Barbara stole a glance between the curtain panels at the window. So much wind and rain all day, and now the sun worked hard shooting rays in between the remaining clouds, bullying its way through the chaos.

Chaos. Remembering Teo's behavior at the wedding, she shivered and wrapped arms around her chest, protective as a mother lion, but too late for herself. She had known better when the thought had touched her heart more than a week before the wedding. Still, she had played Teo's game of cat and mouse; she'd even supplied her own trap by walking alone after dark. How foolish. Now, staying the extra week or so with the Judges, her humiliation couldn't be hidden. Just thinking about the *tussle,* as Mr. Judge had called it, warmed her face. Tussle. Fine word for Jackson charging to her rescue, fists flying and blood boiling.

Grabbing the sweater she left on the back of the vanity chair, she stopped and stared in the mirror. A look at the red-eyed girl reminded her to keep her opinions to herself and to trust her upbringing. Her mother would be appalled at the way she'd behaved.

God, I am so sorry for the trouble I caused. Not only am I ashamed, but I let my parents down. I'm even more ashamed I let You down. Please forgive me, and allow me the strength to hold my head up and behave in a manner that will make me proud to be Your child.

There, like Mama taught her. She'd asked for forgiveness. *Done and done.* People, not God, held grudges. She understood He had already forgotten her sins. As far as the east was from the west.

Down the stairs and into the kitchen, her feet carried her lightly to Mrs. Judge's side where she offered a hug before asking, "May I help with dinner?"

"You look better after that nap, now, don't you?" Mrs. Judge returned the hug and stepped away. "Much better, really. We know you miss your folks, but we surely are happy you're here with us a few more days. Helps to get us over missing Betty some, you know?"

Her wistful smile spoke volumes to Barbara about how much they missed their girl. Mrs. Judge added, "How about getting some of the leftover chicken from the icebox? Oh, lands. I still can't seem to call that Philco a refrigerator, can I?" She turned with hands on hips. "Let's make chicken salad sandwiches on crusty rolls and you can bring up some of my bread and butter pickles from the cellar. Ooh, and pickled beets, too. Sound good?"

"Sounds wonderful. I especially love the pickled beets. Yours are even better than Auntie Ina's."

Mrs. Judge blushed. "Oh, pshaw!"

"But don't you ever tell Auntie that, if you meet her. Might hurt her feelings."

"Secret's good with me."

It was hard to look Mrs. Judge in the face without re-membering the mess with Teo, but no sense crying over spilled milk. She laughed at herself as she lifted the pitcher of milk from the front of the refrigerator.

"What's so funny, missy?" Mrs. Judge gazed in Bar-bara's eyes and grinned the way Barbara had seen her do with Betty and Will.

"Nothing. Just remembering some of Mama's advice about spilled milk."

Mrs. Judge reached for the pitcher and platter of chicken, setting them on the counter. Then she took Bar-bara by her hands. "We all make errors. The trick is to never repeat them, just what we've learned from them."

Chapter 15

Lively conversation returned to the dinner table. Everyone but Barbara and Jackson laughed and talked all at once, the family's good nature the best seasoning for leftovers. Barbara didn't look Jackson in the face, though she saw him from the corner of her eye; he didn't shoot a look in her direction, either. Just dipped his head, ate his sandwich and drank his coffee.

The entire world, save Barbara and Jackson, seemed happy. She glanced up and finally caught him exchanging a stolen moment with her, but he immediately looked away, presumably to take another bite of the blackberry pound cake.

She could have been fooling herself all along. Maybe he didn't care. She thought he had loved her and she had tried to force him into admitting the truth. But perhaps he had meant what he had said when he had confessed to her that she was nothing more than his kid sister's best friend. Maybe the kiss had simply happened because she had surprised him in sleep.

Oh, he winks at everyone. Isn't that what Betty had told her? And here she sat like a silly schoolgirl, reading more into the gesture.

Dabbing at her mouth, putting on her friendliest smile, she said, "If you'll all excuse me. I'll do the dishes. I'm going to take Will up on his offer to borrow his bike. Now the rain's stopped, I'd love a ride while everything's so fresh and sweet. Thank you for the lovely dinner, Mrs. Judge. I'll go start on the kitchen."

Mrs. Judge cocked a look from Barbara to Jackson and back to Barbara again. Her brow lifted ever so slightly. "Just run along. I'll get the dishes."

Later, when she opened her bedroom door to leave, she ran smack into an embarrassed Jackson loping along the hallway. "Sorry," he mumbled, eyes focusing on the floor. "I thought you'd left."

"N-no." She tried to smile, but her lips wouldn't coop-erate. "I—I had to change first." The phony smile poked its head through and she felt like crawling in a hole.

The edge of his mouth lifted, just a bit, as if he, too, were trying to be congenial but failing. "If I'm to be hon-est, you look lovely in slacks. Better than any man I've known." Strained laughter forced its way to the surface. "Maybe the look will catch on…in time."

"Thank you. If you'll excuse me, I think I'll go for that ride. The sun's coming out and maybe I'll see a rainbow. Everything's sparkling with raindrops. Nice time for a bike ride." She rambled—couldn't quit talking. "After all this rain, there will be even more flowers blooming. Won't that smell nice?" Her feet didn't cooperate. She stood like a fool, legs thick and heavy.

Jackson stepped aside to let her pass. "Don't let me keep you."

* * *

Why don't you ask her to stay? Better yet, borrow Dad's bike and go with her. Do something. Stop acting like a brainless fool and follow her! You might not get another chance. The good Lord isn't going to give you two natural disasters in one week to help you out.

He followed her down the stairs, hanging back just enough so he wouldn't look too conspicuous. If she turned right now, he'd go along. He followed another second and then thought, if she said, "Go with me" right now, then he'd go. She didn't do that, either.

Stopping on her way to the door, she grabbed her heavier sweater off the hall tree. "You still there?"

"Well, you see, I—"

"I need a bit of fresh air. But the sky looks overcast again."

She tugged at a curl of hair looping near her tiny pearl earring. He longed to reach out and tuck it behind her ear so he could feel the softness one more time. "Here, let me help you with your sweater." *Tell her how you feel.*

"Thank you."

Ask her if you can go along.

No, it wouldn't be right. Anything more would give her the wrong impression.

She turned to leave.

Who was he kidding? He loved this woman. Perhaps she'd be able to love him, too, ghosts and all.

Stop second guessing. Just ask! "Barbara?"

She whirled around too quickly and glanced up. A hopeful breath preceded her voice. "Yes?"

Then a frown deepened those beautiful blue eyes.

She held her hand out. "What, Jackson?" Her eyes narrowed on his face. His scars?

"Be careful. Looks like rain again."

* * *

The breeze blowing fresh, balmy, aromatic air against her face beckoned Barbara to ride a short while longer despite the clouds building anew behind her. Maybe they'd pass over and she could go on riding all evening. Never have to go back. Never have to face Jackson again.

Who was she kidding? He was in her blood, surging straight to the heart each time they met; in her mind, he filled every thought with his face, his words. He threatened to unnerve her each time they were in the same room, and that was no way to live. As soon as possible, she would pack her bag and head home.

Barbara stopped the bike, wrapped her arms around herself in a big hug and stared into the dusky evening. She should head back. Where was she, exactly? She'd left the town proper some time ago. The factory was on Main and she'd changed her mind and turned left, farther out of town. So, two roads down from Main. Or had she gone three? One more road over and she'd be at the school—kindergarten to high school all in one building. She should now be on one of the roads parallel to and behind the peanut factory.

Another look at the clouds convinced her, ready or not, time to head for cover.

If she shot through the field, instead of staying on the main drag, she'd end up behind the factory shaving about a mile off the return trip. A rumble of thunder made her mind up for her.

Will did say he cut through on his way home from school from time to time, especially when he was running late for work. It couldn't be too difficult to maneuver.

A drop of rain plopped into her face. Then another and another. Just a light drizzle, but enough for a soaking if she didn't hurry. Before she could pedal harder, lightning cracked overhead and thunder rolled.

Well, God hadn't intervened as Jackson had asked.

They'd simply think he went to sleep and when he didn't come to the door in the morning, they'd figure he was being obstinate. If they knocked, no one would bother until it was too late. He'd played this game for so long, nobody expected much from him other than seclusion.

Passing the restroom, he stopped, opened the huge wooden medicine chest and took out the bottle of aspirin. Turning it in his hand, he accepted that God hadn't let him know he was still needed. So, he had the okay to go ahead like the coward he was.

Forgive me, Father. I'm sorry I've let You down at every turn. And I'm sorry I've blamed You. I have no one to blame for my failures other than myself. I'll ask this one last thing. Give them comfort. While I've failed so many people, I just can't go on like this any longer without Your help, and once again, You've said no.

Jackson set down the bottle of aspirin on his nightstand.

He strode to the window and watched the clouds rolling overhead. A few drops of rain pelted the roof of the shed outside. Another storm. Where was she? Drat! The woman could irritate a saint. She must still be out and about and she was going to get caught in one humdinger of a storm. He started to pray. No, he didn't have the right, but Barbara was in danger; he sensed it.

Father, I don't even have the right to ask, but help me. Please. Give me the strength to find her. I can't lose another person so dear to my life. Please, help me.

As lightning struck above the house, he rose and dashed down the stairs where he met his mother at the bottom step just starting up, Barbara's coat in her hand.

"Jackson, I was just about to call up to your room. Would you mind? I'm afraid Barbara might have been caught in the storm. Poor little thing's probably soaked through, don't you think?" His mother's worried expression confirmed his apprehension.

"I'll take the car."

As he pushed against the wind to open the car door, his mother shouted from the stoop. "Will said she headed across the road. She told him she was headed west. Start that direction, all right?"

I know when you're near me.

What a stupid thing to have said. But would he really know if she were in trouble? Near enough for him to be able to locate her? He slammed his foot to the pedal as another streak shot across the sky. The thunder sounded, sooner this time.

His chest compressed until the breath came shallow and fast. He couldn't feel her presence. But he had no choice other than to keep looking. She was out there—alone.

Barbara fought to push the bike through the mud. No use. She dropped it and ran for cover. A bolt of lightning hit a wire bale. She recognized the factory. Next to the loading dock, she cringed against the side of a building, her arms over her head. Horizontal rain soon filled her eyes, her mouth, every piece of her clothing. So cold, her teeth chattered, and her arms hugged her for warmth. No good. Alone and afraid, she huddled in a squat position, praying someone would come along. She pressed into the wooden wall until her feet slipped in the squishy mud. Down with a splat!

What if no one found her?

Barbara shivered. Her arms tightened. Lightning

crashed right next to her and she screamed, but the wind screamed louder.

The rain chilled her inside and out, pelting her like sharp, wet needles. *Lord, please help me. I'm stranded outside in this storm and I'm cold. Very cold. How long can a person stay so cold?* Home was just around the corner, but she couldn't stand against the howling wind. She crawled through the mud to get closer to the back door. Hanging onto the metal handle, she crouched beneath the overhang; still head-rattling wind pummeled her so that she couldn't move.

Every few minutes, Jackson stopped and tried to let the car lights shine into the darkness. He drove up Pennyman, in case she'd gone to visit Aunt Jenny and Mary Anne. In front of the house, he jumped from the car, ran up the steps to the porch and pounded on the door.

"Goodness, Jackson. What is it? You'll scare a body to death. Come in out of the storm. We heard on the radio they spotted a tornado just west of us."

"Is Barbara here? She's missing."

Aunt Jenny shook her head, frowned, mirrored his concern as her own. "No. Lands, where could she have gone? Well, if she does show up," his aunt promised, "I'll tell her to skedaddle right home." Worry dotted her face. "On second thought. I'll make her come and take shelter with us 'til this passes."

"Thanks." He leaped from the porch and ran for the car. With the door barely closed, he revved the engine and tore away toward town.

Once he'd covered the entire downtown area, he left for a search of the back roads. His headlights reflected in all directions. No sign of Barbara. People don't simply disappear. She had to know Mother and Father would be worried sick. Unable to see through the rain and darkness any longer, he pulled the car to the side of the road, stopped the engine and listened. All he could hear was the shrieking storm, like thousands of demons. Where was she? Any person with an ounce of common sense was home out of the storm.

His vision might be hindered, but his instincts told him that he should be somewhere near the huge loading port behind the peanut factory. Could she have tried to ride out the weather there? Jackson jumped out of the car and ran in that general direction. A loud explosion, and the tree in front of him split from a lightning strike. He had to find her.

Praying as he ran, Jackson struggled against the wind. *Father, did you bring me out here? Is this how You're answering my prayer? I know I haven't exactly been the star pupil in Your class, but I'm not asking for myself. Please, keep Barbara safe. I have no idea where she is, but You do. Forgive me for being such a jerk, for even thinking of taking my life. But if You'll give me another chance, I promise this, I will serve You all the remaining days of my life. And I will keep that promise no matter what happens to me, to my family, or even to Barbara. She's Yours, Lord. I trust You with her. Now, please, help me to find her.*

He stopped, gazed in all directions. Where was he? He couldn't see a thing.

He had to find the factory in this blinding storm. It was the only logical place for her to take shelter. That, or she could be home already slipping into dry clothes, Mother hovering with a cup of hot tea and plenty of towels. He pictured her there in front of the fireplace. *Please let her be home.*

Wiping rain from his eyes as he ran, Jackson smelled

the rain, hoping for a scent of the factory. Anything to tell him where he was. *Barbara, where on earth are you?*

Barbara clawed at the door. Pounded for someone to let her in. Pieces of metal and scraps of wood from the loading area spun in the air. She drew closer to the building. A thud next to her head dropped her flat to the ground. A large sign had broken off the back of the storage shack and just missed her head. She scrambled toward the back of the shed. Would the door open?

Her fingers dug at the handle, but a lock kept her from safety.

Father, I need help. You can calm seas, please calm this storm. Send someone to get me out of here. Protect me, Lord.

Her next push on the door popped the lock. She crept in, out of the rain, out of the cold, but before she could get comfortable, the door broke free of its hinges. As her eyes adjusted to the darkness, she gazed upward. Tools, all sorts of tools and shipping crates wobbled over her head. Now what? If she went out, she risked being hit by flying debris; if she stayed in, she might be battered with the tools.

Arms over her head, she fell against her knees. Sobs poured from her throat, raw from crying. Why had she been such a fool? She'd been raised to be sensible and somehow, once she had arrived in New Hope, all that training had been set aside. And here she was caught between the danger inside and the danger outside.

Hearing a loud pop, she looked up. The window above her splintered into hundreds of pieces and showered down on her. A stack of wood crates teetered to the side, then fell, blocking the door. A scream ripped from her throat.

* * *

Jackson cocked his head. A woman's scream. He forced his legs forward, his back burning with each step. He could see it now. The factory was just ahead.

Wooden pallets had loosened from their moorings; now broken slats littered the loading dock. The awning, jerked from the building at one end, swayed back and forth in front of the back door.

Too exhausted to walk any farther in the mud and debris, his strength zapped by fighting the wind, too, Jackson tried to keep his footing, but slipped in the mud and cracked his head on the shack.

"Help! Is someone there? I'm trapped in here! Help me!"

He hauled himself up. Barbara! Thank God.

In no time at all, he crawled around the building and found her stuck behind a few hundred pounds of wood and metal crates. He cleared them one at a time until he saw her face. Instead of fear, a faint smile tipped her lips. Not waiting for her to move, he tugged her into his arms.

"What took you so long?"

Chapter 16

After a hot bath, Barbara, her legs covered in a warm, woolly shawl, sipped tea by the fire next to Mrs. Judge who hovered. "Really, I'm fine. Thank you so much for your concern. If I hadn't been so foolish in the first place—"

"Shush. You're safe. That's all that matters, dear." Mrs. Judge offered another shortbread cookie. "Here, you need to keep up your strength."

She smiled. Just like her own mother would do.

Jackson helped his father put more wood on the fire, turned and smiled at her. "Feeling better?"

She lifted the shawl over her arms and snuggled under the softness. "A little. I've never been so happy to see anyone in my entire life."

"I'm thankful I had the key to the factory on me. We would never have made it home."

Her eyes grew heavy in the light of the fire. Jackson's voice comforted her until she felt stronger. Warm, at last.

Then she thought of Jackson slipping in the mud, hitting his head on the side of the building. No wonder he found her tedious. She seemed to be the cause of so much trouble for him.

She pulled the shawl from around her and rose from the sofa. As she walked over to Jackson, she drew a hankie from the pocket of her slacks. "Here. Maybe we should see to your cuts."

Mrs. Judge started to her feet, looked Barbara in the eyes and nodded. She reached for the cups. "I'll clean up."

Barbara *could* be a little more careful. If she wanted to. Jackson sat on the kitchen chair as quietly as possible so the cleaning and bandaging wouldn't hurt so much. "Ouch."

"Oh, don't be such a big baby." She sponged the area under his eye and then tackled the dried blood as he reached up and touched his upper lip.

"It hurts."

"Jackson, sit still. You're being difficult."

"Maybe a little sympathy's in order. After all, I found you and brought you home." She actually seemed to be taking pleasure in torturing him.

"Stop. I'm not hurting anyone. This Mercurochrome only stings a tad. And can't possibly hurt as much as the side of the factory did when your hard head met it. Face-to-face."

Thank You, God. She hasn't lost her sassy sense of humor. Thank You. I mean it. You led me right to her.

For the first time since Pearl, Jackson felt connected to God in a way he hadn't even known when he had left. He trusted Him with his entire life. For good, for bad, from here on out.

"You think—" he gestured to his battered face "—this is funny?"

"I think *you* are funny. Always have. That first time when you flirted with me through the window of my father's car. Then when you trapped me under the mistletoe. Oh, you're funny all right." Her eyes crinkled at the edges, tugging at his heart.

"Here," he said. Had she really meant what she had said to him? Did she really love him? He had to give it a try. Had to be sure it was love and not merely pity she felt.

"Here what?" She squinted, stared as he pointed. "You're cut there. Let me get a bandage on and pull the edges together." She cut a swathe of gauze.

"Don't bother with that. Look. This spot." He pointed to his chin, his heart thudding louder than the thunder. "Feel like I was kicked by a mule."

"You've been kicked by mules?" she teased.

"You know what I mean." His hand sweated; he rubbed it against his slacks and then touched his finger to his chin once again. "Maybe if you kissed right here." He waited, his heart doing its best to break out of his ribs.

Barbara leaned back enough to be eye level with him. "Let me see. Oh my, yes, that cut does look bad. Not the kind to fix with a bandage, at all. You poor thing." Her lips brushed the edge of his face. "That better?"

"Much." His breath hitched.

Her eyes flitted over his face, inch by inch. She blinked. "And here." Her hand slid gently over his eye. "This looks awful. Must be the side of the building jumped right out and hit you." She kissed his forehead, but he could tell she avoided the worst of his swollen brow by kissing over the top of his injury from Pearl.

He swallowed hard. She wasn't afraid of his scars.

"And here?" He indicated the cut above his lip, which had swollen right away.

"Where?"

He longed to wrap his arms around her but was afraid to stop the moment.

She followed his hand. "I see. Right above your lip. Yes, that really does look painful, Jackson." Her fingertips, like feathers, caressed his mouth.

Her head dipped, and she touched her lips to his ever so gently. "That the right spot?"

He couldn't refrain another second. Lifting his arms, he drew her onto his lap and enclosed her in a tight embrace. Pain or no pain, his lips found hers before she could take a breath. With more love than he figured he deserved in an entire lifetime, she kissed him back. Softly, gently, but with purpose. A kiss that told him she would accept no more excuses about who he was or what he looked like.

Barbara thought he'd kiss the air right out of her. Now *that* was a kiss worth waiting for. Protected, safe, secure—loved for the very first time by a man other than her father. She snuggled against his chest. He nestled his face into her neck, the pulse at that very spot pounding out its rhythm. Then she opened her eyes and stared into the handsomest face she'd ever seen, blood, scars and all.

"I hope you'll let me stay here a while. I sort of like the feel of your arms around me."

His lips attempted a smile, but with the swelling, a lopsided grin that drove a velvety stake through her heart emerged instead. "Understand one thing. I'm no VanDusen."

"Thank goodness. I want more than just a name." She straightened and stared into his eyes. "Jackson, do you think we could talk later tonight? I mean, *really* talk."

"How about if you finish patching me up, and then we'll do anything you like." He let his eyebrows lift up and down until she slapped his arm.

After his folks had retired for the night and he was no longer chilled through to his muscles, he pulled Barbara next to him on the sofa, the fireplace softening the room with a calming light. The only words he could say were, "It's time."

Her smiled curled into his heart, turned two or three times and found a comfortable spot—for both of them.

"Time for what, Jack?"

"I like when you call me Jack. Just never Jackie. Promise? If only Bets knew how irritating that nickname is."

"I won't call you Jackie, and I promise I'll never tell her. She loves you so."

His arm slipped around her shoulder and he pulled her as close as they could get. This was not going to be easy. "Can you…I mean…will you be able to listen to what I say?"

Barbara touched his cheeks with the palms of her hands, avoiding the bruises. He allowed the softness to put him at ease.

Her eyes met his. "About Pearl Harbor? I can listen to anything you want to tell me." She surprised him by casually planting a kiss on his jaw. "Or would you rather wait 'til another time?"

"No. I've waited long enough." Muscles twitching, his face tightened at the thought of Pearl. "I've tried to hide the reality from myself for so long, I'm not sure where to start. The black-and-white reels couldn't capture the horror of that day."

"Jack, just start at the beginning."

He closed his eyes, breathed out air that felt like it had

been trapped in his lungs since that day when he had held his breath, diving under the water. Time and again. "I'll tell you from the first second I can remember." He sucked back, steadied his breath, calmed his heart rate.

"I was sleeping following midwatch, that's night duty, and I awoke to the sound of a huge blast. It came from somewhere starboard, near the bow. Then sirens followed a couple more bursts of noise. Most of us figured another drill, and we pulled the covers over our heads. But after that first small blast came a deafening roar port bow."

When her face crinkled in confusion, he said, "That means the front of the ship. One gigantic explosion and the message, 'Air raid, Pearl Harbor. This is not a drill,' told us to get a move on. Then the call to General Quarters. We flew from our racks, pulling on clothes as we ran outside unprepared for what we'd see.

"Dozens, no hundreds of men jumped into the water while thick gray smoke blanketed the harbor. A deep, continuous buzz streamed overhead and when we squinted through the smoke, a mass of planes flew above us like a well-disciplined flock of geese with one thing in mind— their mission. The meatballs on the fuselage and wings—" he stopped, knowing she wouldn't have a clue "—the large red circles on the sides of the planes were so close you could almost reach out and touch 'em if you tried. No one was sure what they meant at first. But in no time, we understood it was the rising sun of the Japanese flag.

"Ollie, who'd been on days, ran across the deck toward me, screaming for us to get off the ship. One minute he was next to me—right next to me. I looked him in the eyes. He was there and in a millisecond, he was gone. The deck collapsed at the very spot where he stood and he pitched forward, plunging into the water. I grabbed the rail and hung on by sheer will. By then, even though only seconds had passed, oil and debris from numerous ships covered the harbor. Some patches burned. Others were simply thick pools of the ships' lifeblood. All I could see of Ollie was his face looking up with those big googly eyes. He tried to paddle but went under. Up again, he screamed, 'Help me, Jack. I can't swim.'

"I had to reach him, but at the moment, he seemed a mile away. If I jumped and hit the debris, I'd be gone and he wouldn't have anyone to save him. Men were shouting on either side of him, 'Open the lockers and throw the vests! Get us out! Over here.' You couldn't look in any direction without seeing a mass of men, burning, crying, shouting for rescue."

Barbara placed her hand over his, her voice merely a whisper. "I'm so sorry. I had no idea how bad it was."

Jackson choked down tears. "My dilemma was immediately resolved. A man came barreling at me from behind and both of us were catapulted into the water. I hit my back on a sheet of metal going in and then it bobbed back up in the water, crossing over me, cutting my face. Ollie, now hanging on to a wooden plank, watched in horror. The water from my entry drove straight up in the air and struck him in the face, driving his glasses from his nose and him from the board.

"'Jack! Don't leave me here, I'll die.' Then the metal sheet clobbered him in the skull. He shot under a second time. When he came up again, water shot from his mouth as he gulped in air. 'Save me, Jack!' I'd tried to teach him to swim on at least a dozen occasions while we were docked. How does a guy who can't swim get in the navy?

"I reached out and grabbed him, but he slipped through my fingers. I thought I had him by his tags, but they broke loose from the weight and the way I'd wrenched him, trying to grab hold. I got the tags and a chunk of his shirt.

"By then, oil covered my arms and a bit of my neck. I saw flames lick at the water not twenty or so feet from me. I was holding my breath, diving, returning to the surface, diving again. But no Ollie. I held it so long I thought my lungs would burst.

"Hands grabbed me from behind, slapping at my skin. That's when I noticed the oil burning on my arms and hands. Then two men lifted me into a raft."

He couldn't help it, his line of vision settled on the worst of his scars. Then he shivered, hating the expression he saw on Barbara's face.

"Men died everywhere that day, Barbara. You could reach a hand in any direction and find a man choking back his last breath. You can read about hell in the Bible, but we lived through it. Fire burned on the ships, in the water, in buildings, on the land. It covered men's entire bodies. No matter where you looked, there was burning and devastation. There wasn't a single place you could go to escape the sweltering heat."

Barbara turned her head aside, and he caught a glimpse of her drawing a hand toward her eyes. He wished with all his might he wasn't causing her this pain. "Are you sure you want to hear the rest of this?"

"Jackson, if you talk about what happened, you'll begin to heal. To put it behind you."

"I s'pose."

She brushed hair from the cut on his forehead. "With all that you went through, why do you blame yourself for your friend's death?"

He pulled his arm from around her shoulder and straightened, almost militarily. "Ollie. He trusted me to take care of him. He was only seventeen, Barbara. A kid whose parents waited at home for the call or telegram that would say: *The President of the United States and the Secretary of the Navy regret to inform you that your son was killed in action on December 7, 1941. Please accept the thanks of a grateful nation.* Or something equally mundane."

"Where did they take you?"

Her face blurred before his eyes. "I hardly remember. Guy Stryker had me in his arms like a baby, running through what had been a street leading to the hospital. By that time, the sun tried to push through the smoke, and just the hint of it on my arms scorched like a blow torch. Men around me rushed toward the hospital to get help for their friends, some already dead in their arms." He choked back tears.

Barbara reached out and he wanted to pull her close, but the memories separated them.

"Jackson, I'm so sorry," she said.

"No one could have known what would happen. And if they had, they couldn't have stopped it. God help the men who died there, and more importantly, those who didn't. They'll have to live with the memories like me."

She pressed fingers over his rough, scarred hand. "I didn't realize." What else could she say? Try as she might, she would never understand what Jackson and the others had endured. But now, after talking about it, she could see a change in his demeanor. He would always carry the emotional scars, but at least he was willing to try and get past this.

Silent now, he sucked his lower lip in, biting down.

He turned, looked her direction. "Oliver was barely older than my brother, you know. A kid with his entire life in front of him."

"Oliver?"

Jackson's fingers steepled. He slumped against the sofa back, closed his eyes.

She caught herself holding her breath, afraid to let it out and break the silence, but she asked again, "Oliver? I thought you said Ollie."

"Yeah, Oliver McHale. My rack mate. We all called him Ollie. Should have called him Owlie. He had these big eyes that looked even bigger behind his Coke-bottle glasses. Probably wouldn't have taken him in the navy if we hadn't been headed for war."

McHale? "Oliver McHale?"

He opened his eyes and crooked his neck to the side. "Yes. Why?"

"He's alive, Jack."

He sat straight, gripped her wrist, his face contorted. "I don't know if you're trying to console me, but…"

She lifted palms to his chest. His heart beat strong through the shirt. "It's not a joke. I rode on the train with his mother. She and Mr. McHale had been to see him. He's still in the hospital, but he's alive, Jackson. She said it took a while for them to identify him. No tags." She tried to stop her grin from spreading, felt it fan out and cover her face.

He tugged her head onto his chest and buried his face in her neck. "I don't know what to say. For more than five months I've harbored the notion…now you tell me Ollie's alive. I feel like hopping the first train."

Barbara lifted her head and wrapped her arms around him. They sat, intertwined for over an hour, neither one of them speaking, only the soft breathing and the echo of two hearts beating as one. When, at last, he raised his head, his eyes had filled and he didn't even try to brush the tears away. "Barbara, I'm so ashamed."

"Ashamed?"

"If I told you what I'd planned."

"Planned for what, Jack?"

"For after Betty's wedding. God forgive me for even contemplating anything so selfish."

"Jackson? You don't need to say another word." She didn't move, didn't dare.

"Tonight I want to hold you as long as you'll let me here on the couch, then go upstairs and climb into my bed." He grinned. "And sleep. For the first time in five months, I plan to sleep. And Barbara?"

With hope spilling out of control, she smiled. "Yes?"

His voice—husky and full of love—caressed her like a piece of fine silk. "No more running off. My poor old body can't take it."

She squeezed tighter. "Oh, Jackson."

"Jack. I like when you call me Jack."

"Whatever you like, Jack. Just kiss me."

Chapter 17

Jackson popped the last bite of warm sticky bun in his mouth and swigged coffee from his cup. Holding it out, he smiled at his mother. "A little more cream?" She plopped a dollop into the cup. "Thanks. I really didn't expect you to get up and bake so early."

"It's time we fattened you up a bit. Here, have another."

"I've gotten fat and lazy as it is."

"Oh, lands, boy. You need pick on those bones. May have muscle still, but we need to fill you out again, don't we?"

He smiled. All seemed right in his world for the first time in a very long while.

His mother patted his hand. "Barbara slept in. Poor little thing."

"Thanks for all you've done for her."

She blushed and pushed the platter closer.

"Whoa." Jackson chuckled. "Dad, make her stop. I want

to fill out, not fatten up like this year's Thanksgiving turkey."

"Fiddlesticks."

"I'll have to work all kinds of overtime to keep from getting fat, Mother. Slow down there."

"Are you serious, son?" His father leaned forward, nearly upending his own coffee. "Because Fred's way in over his head at the factory. Even asked me if I'd start to look for another manager so he could step down."

Jackson shook his head. Fred *wasn't* manager material, and they all knew it. "Yeah, about that."

"I think you might be able to put things to right."

Jackson nodded. He loved this house. Loved these people. How had he allowed himself to become so caught up in his own misery? Last night he had seen some of the first good sleep he'd had since coming home, but he hadn't slept long. For much of the night he had spent in prayer. Reconnecting with the Father who hadn't let him down after all. *There is a reason for everything that happens. Father, how could I have doubted You?*

Never again would he allow the doubts to consume him in such a destructive manner.

"Why are you staring? Aren't I just about the handsomest man you've ever seen?" He clipped his mother under the chin.

She reached out and patted the side of his face like she'd done a hundred times when he was a child. "You are that. And then some." Her eyes traveled to his father. "Just like your handsome daddy. You all right, son?"

"I'll be fine now." Should he broach the subject? "And I think *she* will, too. If I ever get around to asking her." He raised his brow, hinting at his intentions.

His mother pushed the pan of buns aside and threw her arms around his neck. "I'm so happy for you, son."

He threw his head back and laughed aloud. "Don't put the horse before the cart, dear lady. I haven't made it official yet. You and Father are the only ones who know I'm going to pop the question. Mum's the word. Don't say anything to Will. Especially not Will."

"There's something in my sewing basket I have to get."

"What's that?"

Barbara stretched and looked at the clock on the nightstand. Seven o'clock? She'd slept in. The entire family must be at the table. She dashed from the cozy bed, hurried to wash and dress. Patting her hair into place, as much as she could control the loosely permed curls, she took a parting glance in the mirror. Not good, but not bad for being in such a rush. She slipped down the stairs and peeked into the dining room. Mr. and Mrs. Judge stared her direction.

Uh-oh. Mrs. Judge's face had an odd expression. Could she be upset Barbara was late?

Jackson's back was to her. "Good morning, Barbara."

Goose bumps covered her. How did he do that? "Good morning, everyone. Sorry I overslept. You should have gone ahead without me."

Mrs. Judge nodded. "We did, dear."

Barbara smelled the cinnamon and recognized the gooey sticky buns of which she was so fond. "Mmm. I think my nose carried me down here just in time. Wouldn't want to miss out on a sticky bun."

Mrs. Judge smiled.

As Barbara pulled out her chair, she said, "I think I've figured out your secret."

Mrs. Judge looked shocked, and Jackson stunned.

"What's that?" she asked.

"You crack the nuts fresh when you make the buns. Am I right?"

A nervous laugh danced through her lips. "Oh, right. Yes, my mother taught me that. And we all know what a great cook Mrs. Delaney was."

"She was that. Could you pass one of the rolls?" They all gave her an odd once-over.

Jackson turned, offered a stern look, then returned to the food on his plate. What was wrong with him this morning? Maybe he was embarrassed he'd confided in her.

He rose from the table. "When you finish eating, we need to talk."

"A-all right." Did she see a smile crease Mrs. Judge's face? No. Must be a scowl.

His heart had been working overtime lately, tripping constantly. And now proved no different. He shook all over. As he plopped his dish in the sink, he looked at his hands and couldn't believe how they trembled, like some little kid's.

What if she said no?

Stop second-guessing. Just wait to see what she decides.

Jackson entered the dining room and winked at his mother. "Are you finished with breakfast?"

Barbara swiped a napkin over her face. She nodded to his parents. "If you'll excuse me." When her eyes met Jack's, the look was so questioning. "Let me grab my sweater in case it's cool out."

Once she returned from her room, he helped her into the sweater and they stepped off the porch in sync. His hand brushed her arm lightly, steering her away from the house.

She had to stretch to keep up with his strides, but he continued at the nervous, frenzied pace.

Out of the corner of his eye, he examined her, searching for one inkling of what she might say. The rest of his life depended on that answer.

* * *

"What did you want to discuss, Jack?" Her eyes focused on the sidewalk, careful to stay out of the mud. For some reason she didn't feel her usual confident self. And he seemed upset. Maybe bringing up the past last night had caused the terrible nightmares to return.

Once they reached the end of the road, they headed toward higher ground. When they hit an open field, high above the town, he stopped and dropped the blanket he had tucked under his arm.

Barbara's stomach flopped over and over like the seats of a giant, tumbling Ferris wheel. "Jack, what is it?"

"Please. Sit down." He indicated the brown wool blanket.

He looked so serious. "What's happened? Are you all right?"

"I have to ask you something and I'm not sure how well this will sit with you."

"Ask. Please." She wouldn't tell anyone about what he had shared with her. He should know that without asking. "Is something wrong?"

He caught the edge of his lip between his teeth and the frown dipped deeper than before.

"It'll only be wrong if you say no."

What? Her voice quivered. "Then ask."

Jackson took a deep breath and held it as he slipped to one knee next to her. She knew from the strained look on his face the effort came at a cost. Dropping his hand into his pocket, he drew out an exquisite gold ring, on closer inspection, a circle of tiny pearls outlining a rather large diamond. "Well, I'm not sure you know it, but the Arts Society in Chattanooga is discussing an opera house. Dad told me the church choir director mentioned it to him."

"You brought me out here to tell me about Chatta-nooga?"

"No. Yes. Well, sort of. Listen, Barbara. I know I'm no prize at the carnival, but you've made me believe I'm not the circus freak show anymore, either. I'm honest with myself about how I appear to other people, but for whatever reason, you choose to see a different man than who I see in the mirror. You could do a lot better, much better, ten times better, but here I am, on bended knee. This was my grandmother's ring. What I'm trying to say is, Barbara Richardson, will you honor me?"

She blinked. "*Honor* you?"

"Marry me. I promise to wake up every morning and thank God you were brought into my life. And I'll fall asleep each night with you in my arms, thanking God he delivered me so I'm able to appreciate your love. And I'll never try to rob you of your dreams. Never. If you don't mind keeping your career in Tennessee, that is."

Barbara blinked, finding herself tongue-tied. She opened her mouth to say yes, but nothing came out. No *yes*. No squawk. No squeak. No sarcasm. Nothing. She shifted on the blanket to give herself time to recover her thoughts. Swallowing hard over a lump so dry she nearly choked, she fought to catch her breath. *Say something. Anything. Don't just sit here staring at him. This is what you've wanted.*

Jackson looked over at her, his eyes imploring her to answer, but she remained mute. He stood to his feet, Barbara unable to speak or move. He leaned and cupped her chin in his hand. "Does that mean yes or no? 'Cause I'm really doubting myself here."

She licked her lips. Any second now her tongue would free up.

He smiled. "Well, this is surely a first. Barbara Richardson with nothing to say." He made a noise with his tongue and cheek.

Taking her hand, he lifted her to her feet, slipped the ring on her finger, and his eyebrow rose. "You know. In most cultured societies, it's customary for the girl to give the man an answer. Preferably yes, but anything at this point would move us along."

Barbara wrapped her arms around his neck and kissed him. If the words wouldn't come, she'd find some way to say yes. Her face warmed as she buried her cheek against his chest.

He laid a gentle hand against her head, pressing her closer until she could hear the strumming of his heart—the gallop. It was beating as fast as she was sure hers did. Finally, she looked up, eyes full of tears, and said, "Yes, Jack, you big tease. I'll marry you. I'll marry you good."

As he dipped his head slowly, he looked directly into her eyes with so much compassion she nearly lifted off the ground. Instead, she stood quietly subdued while he kissed her. Once, twice, softly, gently, then with a strength that worked its way straight to her heart.

"How soon?" He whispered the words against her lips as his hands ran the length of her arms.

She laughed. "How soon what?"

"Well, even after the storm, the gazebo is standing. Hate to waste all that hard work. And Mom's garden is almost in full bloom." He leaned down and kissed her again and again, until all the world faded away. There were only the two of them in the entire universe with New Hope providing the perfect backdrop. "And you did tell me once that you planned to be married this summer."

Even though she'd loved him for so long, her heart made room for knowing he loved her back.

Barbara opened her eyes in time to catch that smug

look reappearing on his face as if he knew from the day she had arrived she'd say yes.

"Jackson Judge. You sure do think you're something, don't you?"

* * * * *

REQUEST YOUR FREE BOOKS!

2 FREE CHRISTIAN NOVELS
PLUS 2
FREE
MYSTERY GIFTS

HEARTSONG
PRESENTS

REQUEST YOUR FREE BOOKS!

2 FREE INSPIRATIONAL NOVELS
PLUS 2
FREE
MYSTERY GIFTS

Love Inspired

YES! Please send me 2 FREE Love Inspired® novels and my 2 FREE mystery gifts (gifts are worth about $10). After receiving them, if I don't wish to receive any more books, I can return the shipping statement marked "cancel." If I don't cancel, I will receive 6 brand-new novels every month and be billed just $4.49 per book in the U.S. or $4.99 per book in Canada. That's a savings of at least 22% off the cover price. It's quite a bargain! Shipping and handling is just 50¢ per book in the U.S. and 75¢ per book in Canada.* I understand that accepting the 2 free books and gifts places me under no obligation to buy anything. I can always return a shipment and cancel at any time. Even if I never buy another book, the two free books and gifts are mine to keep forever.

105/305 IDN FVYV

Name _____ (PLEASE PRINT)

Address _____ Apt. #

City _____ State/Prov. _____ Zip/Postal Code

Signature (if under 18, a parent or guardian must sign)

Mail to the Harlequin® Reader Service:
IN U.S.A.: P.O. Box 1867, Buffalo, NY 14240-1867
IN CANADA: P.O. Box 609, Fort Erie, Ontario L2A 5X3

**Are you a subscriber to Love Inspired books
and want to receive the larger-print edition?
Call 1-800-873-8635 or visit www.ReaderService.com.**

* Terms and prices subject to change without notice. Prices do not include applicable taxes. Sales tax applicable in N.Y. Canadian residents will be charged applicable taxes. Offer not valid in Quebec. This offer is limited to one order per household. Not valid for current subscribers to Love Inspired books. All orders subject to credit approval. Credit or debit balances in a customer's account(s) may be offset by any other outstanding balance owed by or to the customer. Please allow 4 to 6 weeks for delivery. Offer available while quantities last.

Your Privacy—The Harlequin® Reader Service is committed to protecting your privacy. Our Privacy Policy is available online at www.ReaderService.com or upon request from the Harlequin Reader Service.
We make a portion of our mailing list available to reputable third parties that offer products we believe may interest you. If you prefer that we not exchange your name with third parties, or if you wish to clarify or modify your communication preferences, please visit us at www.ReaderService.com/consumerchoice or write to us at Harlequin Reader Service Preference Service, P.O. Box 9062, Buffalo, NY 14269. Include your complete name and address.

LIDIR13

HEARTSONG

PRESENTS

Look out for 4 new
Heartsong Presents books next month!

**Every month 4 inspiring faith-filled
romances will be available in stores.**

These contemporary and historical Christian
romances emphasize God's role in every
relationship and reinforce the importance of
faith, hope and love.

Jolie Sheridan gets more than she bargained for when she arrives at Sunrise Ranch for a teaching job.

Read on for a preview of
HER UNFORGETTABLE COWBOY by Debra Clopton.

Jolie followed Morgan outside. There was a large gnarled oak tree still bent over as it had been all those years ago. She didn't stop until she reached it, turning his way only after they were beneath the wide expanse of limbs.

Morgan crossed his arms and studied the tree. "I remember having to climb up this tree and talk you down after you scrambled up to the top and froze."

She hadn't expected him to bring up old memories—it caught her a little off guard. "I remember how mad you were at having to rescue the silly little new girl."

A hint of a smile teased his lips, fraying Jolie's nerves at the edges. It had been a long time since she'd seen that smile.

"I got used to it, though," he said, his voice warming.

Electricity hummed between them as they stared at each other. Jolie sucked in a wobbly breath. Then the hardness in Morgan's tone matched the accusation in his eyes.

"What are you doing here, Jolie? Why aren't you taming rapids in some far-off place?"

"I...I'm—" She stumbled over her words. "I'm taking a leave from competition for a little while. I had a bad run in Virginia." She couldn't bring herself to say that she'd almost died. "Your dad offered me this teaching opportunity."

"I heard about the accident and I'm real sorry about that, Jolie," Morgan said. "But why come here after all this time?"

"This is my *home*."

Jolie saw anger in Morgan's eyes. Well, he had a right to it, and more than a right to point it straight at her.

But she'd thought she'd prepared for it.

She was wrong.

"Morgan," Jolie said, almost as a whisper. "I'd hoped we could forget the past and move forward."

Heart pounding, she reached across the space between them and placed her hand on his arm. It was just a touch, but the feeling of connecting with Morgan McDermott again after so much time rocked her straight to her core, and suddenly she wasn't so sure coming home had been the right thing to do after all.

Will Morgan ever allow Jolie back into
his life—and his heart?

Pick up HER UNFORGETTABLE COWBOY
from Love Inspired Books.

LIEXP0413RR